A GIFT FOR:

____

FROM:

____

DATE:

____

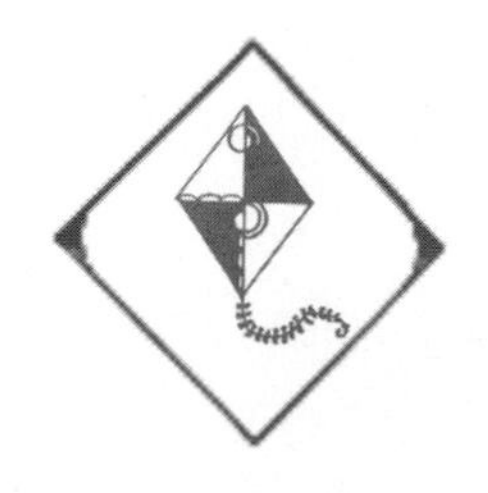

THE NIGHTSTAND READER FOR KIDS

Published by
Hallmark Cards, Inc.
Kansas City, Missouri

BOK1082

Published by Hallmark Cards, Inc., under license from
Mark Gilroy Communications, Inc.

www.hallmark.com

The Nightstand Reader for Kids

6528 E. 101st Street, Suite 416
Tulsa, Oklahoma 74133

Created by Mark K. Gilroy. Compiled by Christina Honea with Mark Gilroy

Cover design and illustration by Thurber Creative Services, Inc.

Illustrations by Karen Eland.

Printed in Thailand

THE NIGHTSTAND READER FOR KIDS

Contents

Welcome to the Nightstand Reader

Ah, it's the end of a busy day.
Were you at school or was this just a play day?
The sun has set.
Is the moon out tonight?

All your friends have gone home.
Don't worry, you will get to see them tomorrow!
You've been told no more TV for the night.

You've had your last snack.
Was it good?
You've washed your hands and face.

Your teeth are brushed.
And now it's time for bed.
Well . . . almost.

Because nighttime, just before sleep time, is the most wonderful time to read a story . . . or two . . . or three.

Maybe you are old enough to do all your own reading now. You will find short stories and long stories; funny poems and serious thoughts; exciting tales and silly nonsense to fill your dreams with wonderful adventures. We hope you enjoy reading every single word in this book.

If mom or dad is reading to you, make sure that they don't skip the good parts. If they are super tired and yawn a lot, you might have to tickle them to wake them up so they read with lots of enthusiasm and many different voices. (Tickling doesn't always work, but a lot of times it does.)

Whether you like your reading filled with adventure or humor, it's time to relax as you turn off all the lights in your room–except the one on your nightstand. That's the same place you will want to keep this book of wonder and fun.

A Note to Young Readers

Is it best to read every word or skip some of them? How about the big words? Or the long stories? (There are only a few in here.)

Kate Douglas Wiggin, a very young girl, happened to be on the same train with the great English author, Charles Dickens. (He wrote books like *Oliver Twist* and *A Christmas Carol* that have been made into movies.) Kate told him that she had read all of his books.

"Bless my soul!" he cried. "Those long thick books, and you such a slip of a thing."

Then she confessed: "Of course I do skip some of the very dull parts once in a while; not the short dull parts, but the long ones."

If a story is very special to you, you will not skip.

What's the best way to know you love a particular book or story? Simple. You finish it.

We hope you will love the stories and poems in this book so much that you read every single word!

The Land of Nod

Robert Louis Stevenson

From breakfast on through all the day
At home among my friends I stay,
But every night I go abroad
Afar into the land of Nod.

All by myself I have to go,
With none to tell me what to do–
All alone beside the streams
And up the mountain-sides of dreams.

The strangest things are there for me,
Both things to eat and things to see,
And many frightening sights abroad
Till morning in the land of Nod.

Try as I like to find the way,
I never can get back by day,
Nor can remember plain and clear
The curious music that I hear.

Spring Morning

A.A. Milne

Where am I going? I don't quite know.
Down to the stream where the king-cups grow–
Up on the hill where the pine-trees blow–
Anywhere, anywhere. *I* don't know.

Where am I going? The clouds sail by,
Little one, baby ones, over the sky.
Where am I going? The shadows pass,
Little ones, baby ones, over the grass.

If you were a cloud, and sailed up there,
You'd sail on water as blue as air,
And you'd see me here in the fields and say:
"Doesn't the sky look green today?"

Where am I going? The high rooks call:
"It's awful fun to be born at all."
Where am I going? The ring-doves coo:

"We do have beautiful things to do."

If you were a bird, and lived on high,
You'd lean on the wind when the wind came by,
You'd say to the wind when it took you away:
"*That's* where I wanted to go today!"

Where am I going? I don't quite know.
What does it matter where people go?
Down to the wood where the blue-bells grow–
Anywhere, anywhere, *I* don't know.

Never Kick a Slipper at the Moon

Carl Sandburg

When a girl is growing up in the Rootabaga Country she learns some things to do, and some things *not* to do.

"Never kick a slipper at the moon if it is the time for the Dancing Slipper Moon–when the slim early moon looks like the toe and the heel of a dancer's foot," was the advice Mr. Wishes, the father of Peter Potato Blossom Wishes, gave to his daughter.

"Why?" she asked him.

"Because your slipper will go straight up, on and on to the moon, and fasten itself on the moon as if the moon is a foot ready for dancing," said Mr. Wishes.

"A long time ago there was one night when a secret word was passed around to all the shoes standing in the bedrooms and closets.

"The whisper of the secret was: 'Tonight all the shoes and the slippers and the boots of the world are going walking without any feet in them. Tonight when those who put us on their feet in the daytime are sleeping in their beds, we all get up and walk and go walking where we walk in the daytime.'

"And in the middle of the night, when the people in the beds were sleeping, the shoes and the slippers and the boots everywhere walked out of the bedrooms and the closets. Along the sidewalks on the streets, up and down stairways, along hallways, the shoes and slippers and the boots tramped and marched and stumbled.

"Some walked pussyfoot, sliding easy and soft just like people in the daytime. Some walked clumping and clumping, coming down heavy on the heels and slow on the toes, just like people in the daytime.

"Some turned their toes in and walked pigeon-toed, some spread their toes out and held their heels in, just like people in the daytime. Some ran glad and fast, some lagged slow and sorry.

"Now there was a little girl in the Village of Cream Puffs who came home from a dance that night. And she was tired from dancing round dances and square dances, one steps and two steps, toe dances and toe and heel dances, dances close up and dances far apart, she was so tired she took off only one slipper, tumbled onto her bed and went to sleep with one slipper on.

"She woke up in the morning when it was yet dark. And she went to the window and looked up in the sky and saw a Dancing Slipper Moon dancing far and high in the deep blue sea of the moon sky.

"'Oh–what a moon–what a dancing slipper of a moon!' she cried with a little song to herself.

"She opened the window, saying again, 'Oh! What a moon!'–and kicked her foot with slipper on it straight toward the moon.

"The slipper flew off and flew up and went on and on and up and up in the moonshine.

"It never came back, that slipper. It was never seen again. When they asked the girl about it she said, 'It slipped off my foot and went up and up and the last I saw of it the slipper was going on straight to the moon.'"

And these are the explanations why fathers and mothers in the Rootabaga Country say to their girls growing up, "Never kick a slipper at the moon if it is the time of the Dancing Slipper Moon when the ends of the moon look like the toe and the heel of a dancer's foot."

Tom Meets Becky

Mark Twain

From *The Adventures of Tom Sawyer*

When Tom reached the little isolated frame schoolhouse, he strode in briskly, with the manner of one who had come with all honest speed. He hung his hat on a peg and flung himself into his seat with businesslike alacrity. The master, throned on high in his great splint-bottom armchair, was dozing, lulled by the drowsy hum of study. The interruption roused him.

"Thomas Sawyer!"

Tom knew that when his name was pronounced in full, it meant trouble.

"Sir!"

"Come up here. Now, sir, why are you late again, as usual?"

Tom was about to take refuge in a lie, when he saw two long tails of yellow hair hanging down a back that he recognized by the electric sympathy of love; and by that form was *the only vacant place* on the girls' side of the school-house. He instantly said:

"I STOPPED TO TALK WITH HUCKLEBERRY FINN!"

The master's pulse stood still, and he stared helplessly. The buzz of study ceased. The pupils wondered if this foolhardy boy had lost his mind. The master said:

"You–you did what?"

"Stopped to talk with Huckleberry Finn."

There was no mistaking the words.

"Thomas Sawyer, this is the most astounding confession I have ever listened to. No mere ferule will answer for this offence. Take off your jacket."

The master's arm performed until it was tired and the stock of switches notably diminished. Then the order followed:

"Now, sir, go and sit with the girls! And let this be a warning to you."

The titter that rippled around the room appeared to abash the boy, but in reality that result was caused rather more by his worshipful awe of his unknown idol and the dread pleasure that lay in his high good fortune. He sat down upon the end of the pine bench and the girl hitched herself away from him with a toss of her head. Nudges and winks and whispers traversed the room, but Tom sat still, with his arms upon the long, low desk before him, and seemed to study his book.

By and by attention ceased from him, and the accustomed school murmur rose upon the dull air once more. Presently the boy began to steal furtive glances at the girl. She observed it, "made a mouth" at him and gave him the back of her head for the space of a minute. When she cautiously faced around again, a peach lay before her. She thrust it away. Tom gently put it back. She thrust it away again, but with less animosity. Tom patiently returned it to its place. Then she let it remain. Tom scrawled on his slate, "Please take it–I got more." The girl glanced at the words, but made no sign. Now the boy began to draw something on the slate, hiding his work with his left hand. For a time the girl refused to notice; but her human curiosity presently began to manifest itself by hardly perceptible signs. The boy worked on, apparently unconscious. The girl made a sort of noncommittal attempt to see, but the boy did not betray that he was aware of it. At last she gave in and hesitatingly whispered:

"Let me see it."

Tom partly uncovered a dismal caricature of a house with two gable ends to it and a corkscrew of smoke issuing from the chimney. Then the girl's interest began to fasten itself upon the work and she forgot everything else. When it was finished, she gazed a moment, then whispered:

"It's nice–make a man."

The artist erected a man in the front yard that resembled a derrick. He could have stepped over the house; but the girl was not hypercritical; she was satisfied with the monster, and whispered:

"It's a beautiful man–now make me coming along."

Tom drew an hourglass with a full moon and straw limbs to it and armed the spreading fingers with a portentous fan. The girl said:

"It's ever so nice–I wish I could draw."

"It's easy," whispered Tom, "I'll learn you."

"Oh, will you? When?"

"At noon. Do you go home to dinner?"

"I'll stay if you will."

"Good–that's a whack. What's your name?"

"Becky Thatcher. What's yours? Oh, I know. It's Thomas Sawyer."

"That's the name they lick me by. I'm Tom when I'm good. You call me Tom, will you?"

"Yes."

Now Tom began to scrawl something on the slate, hiding the words from the girl. But she was not backward this time. She begged to see. Tom said:

"Oh, it ain't anything."

"Yes it is."

"No it ain't. You don't want to see."

"Yes I do, indeed I do. Please let me."

"You'll tell."

"No I won't–deed and deed and double deed won't."

"You won't tell anybody at all? Ever, as long as you live?"

"No, I won't ever tell *any*body. Now let me."

"Oh, *you* don't want to see!"

"Now that you treat me so, I *will* see." And she put her small hand upon his and a little scuffle ensued, Tom pretending to resist in earnest but letting his hand slip by degrees till these words were revealed: *"I love you."*

"Oh, you bad thing!" And she hit his hand a smart rap, but reddened and looked pleased, nevertheless.

Just at this juncture the boy felt a slow, fateful grip closing on his ear, and a steady lifting impulse. In that vise he was borne across the house and deposited in his own seat, under a peppering fire of giggles from the whole school. Then the master stood over him during a few awful moments, and finally moved away to his throne without saying a word. But although Tom's ear tingled, his heart was jubilant.

The Walrus and the Carpenter

Lewis Carroll

The sun was shining on the sea,
Shining with all his might:
He did his very best to make
The billows smooth and bright–
And this was odd, because it was
The middle of the night.

The moon was shining sulkily,
Because she thought the sun
Had got no business to be there

After the day was done–
"It's very rude of him," she said,
"To come and spoil the fun!"

The sea was wet as wet could be,
The sands were dry as dry.
You could not see a cloud, because
No cloud was in the sky:
No birds were flying overhead–
There were no birds to fly.

The Walrus and the Carpenter
Were walking close at hand:
They wept like anything to see
Such quantities of sand:
"If this were only cleared away,"
They said, "it would be grand!"

"If seven maids with seven mops
Swept it for half a year,
Do you suppose," the Walrus said,
"That they could get it clear?"
"I doubt it," said the Carpenter,
And shed a bitter tear.

"O Oysters, come and walk with us!"
The Walrus did beseech.
"A pleasant walk, a pleasant talk,
Along the briny beach:
We cannot do with more than four,
To give a hand to each."

The eldest Oyster looked at him,
But never a word he said:
The eldest Oyster winked his eye,
And shook his heavy head–
Meaning to say he did not choose
To leave the oyster-bed.

But four young Oysters hurried up,
All eager for the treat:
Their coats were brushed, their faces washed,
And this was odd, because, you know,
They hadn't any feet.

Four other Oysters followed them,
And yet another four;
And thick and fast they came at last,

And more, and more, and more–
All hopping through the frothy waves,
And scrambling to the shore.

The Walrus and the Carpenter
Walked on a mile or so,
And then they rested on a rock
Conveniently low:
And all the little Oysters stood
And waited in a row.

"The time has come," the Walrus said.
"To talk of many things:
Of shoes–and ships–and sealing-wax–
Of cabbages–and kings–
And why the sea is boiling hot–
And whether pigs have wings."

"But wait a bit," the Oysters cried,
"Before we have our chat;
For some of us are out of breath,
And all of us are fat!"
"No hurry!" said the Carpenter.
They thanked him much for that.

"A loaf of bread," the Walrus said,
"Is what we chiefly need:
Pepper and vinegar besides
Are very good indeed–
Now, if you're ready. Oysters dear,
We can begin to feed."

"But not on us!" the Oysters cried,
Turning a little blue.
"After such kindness, that would be
A dismal thing to do!"
"The night is fine," the Walrus said.
"Do you admire the view?

"It was so kind of you to come!
And you are very nice!"
The Carpenter said nothing but
"Cut us another slice.
I wish you were not quite so deaf–
I've had to ask you twice!"

"It seems a shame," the Walrus said,
"To play them such a trick.

After we've brought them out so far,
And made them trot so quick!"
The Carpenter said nothing but
"The butter's spread, too thick!"

"I weep for you," the Walrus said:
"I deeply sympathize."
With sobs and tears he sorted out
Those of the largest size,
Holding his pocket-handkerchief
Before his streaming eyes.

"O Oysters," said the Carpenter,
"You've had a pleasant run!
Shall we be trotting home again?"
But answer came there none–
And this was scarcely odd, because
They'd eaten every one."

THE LION AND THE MOUSE

AESOP

Once when a Lion was asleep a little Mouse began running up and down upon him; this soon wakened the Lion, who placed his huge paw upon him, and opened his big jaws to swallow him.

"Pardon, O King," cried the little Mouse. "Forgive me this time and I shall never forget it. Who knows–I may be able to do you a favor one of these days?" The Lion was so tickled at the idea of the Mouse being able to help him that he lifted up his paw and let him go.

Some time after, the Lion was caught in a trap, and the hunters, who desired to take him away alive, tied him to a tree while they went in search of a wagon to carry him on.

Just then the little Mouse happened to pass by, and seeing the sad plight the Lion was in, went up to him and soon gnawed away the ropes that bound the King of the Beasts.

"Was I not right?" said the little Mouse.

Little friends may prove to be great friends.

The Milkmaid and Her Pail

Aesop

Patty the Milkmaid was going to market carrying her milk in a pail on her head. As she went along she began calculating what she would do with the money she would get for the milk.

"I'll buy some fowls from Farmer Brown," said she, "and they will lay eggs each morning, which I will sell to the parson's wife. With the money that I get from the sale of these eggs I'll buy myself a new dress and a little hat; and when I go to market, won't all the young men come up and speak to me! Polly Shaw will be that jealous; but I don't care. I shall just look at her and toss my head like this."

As she spoke she tossed her head back, the pail fell off, and all the milk was spilled. So she had to go home and tell her mother what had occurred.

"Ah, my child," said the mother,

"Do not count your chickens before they are hatched."

Simple Gifts

Traditional

'Tis the gift to be simple,
'Tis the gift to be free.
'Tis the gift to come down
Where we ought to be,
And when we find ourselves
In the place just right,
'Twill be in the valley
Of love and delight.
When true simplicity is gained,
To bow and to bend
We shan't be ashamed,
To turn, turn will be our delight,
Till by turning, turning
We come 'round right.

Rip Van Winkle

Washington Irving

Many years ago in a small, ancient village nestled at the foot of the great Kaatskill mountains, there lived a simple good-natured fellow by the name of Rip Van Winkle. He was a kind neighbor, and an obedient, hen-pecked husband. Indeed, he possessed a meekness of spirit that gained him universal popularity.

He was a great favorite among all the good wives of the village, who took his part in all family squabbles; and never failed, whenever they talked those matters over in their evening gossip, to lay all the blame on Mrs. Van Winkle. The children of the village, too, would shout with joy whenever he approached. He assisted at their sports, made their toys, taught them to fly kites and shoot marbles, and told them long stories of ghosts, witches, and Indians. Whenever he went dodging about the village, he was surrounded by a troop of them, hanging on his skirts, clambering on his back, and playing a thousand tricks on him, and not one dog would bark at him throughout the neighborhood.

The one great flaw in Rip's composition was an overwhelming aversion to all kinds of profitable labor. It could not be from a lack of perseverance–for he would sit on a wet rock, with a rod as long and heavy as a Tartar's lance, and fish all day without complaint, even if he did not receive a single nibble. He would carry a shotgun on his shoulder for hours, trudging through woods and swamps, and up hill and down dale, to shoot a few squirrels or wild pigeons. He would never refuse to assist a neighbor even in the most challenging work, and was seen at all country frolics husking Indian corn, or building stone fences. The women of the village, too, used to employ him to run their errands, and to do such little odd jobs as their less obliging husbands would not do for them. In a word Rip was ready to attend to anybody's business but his own; but when it came to doing family duty, and keeping his farm in order, he found it impossible. His fences were continually falling to pieces; his cow would either go astray, or get among the cabbages, and weeds were sure to grow quicker in his fields than anywhere else. His children, too, were as ragged and wild as if they belonged to nobody. His son, Rip, a child made in his own likeness, was already showing signs of inheriting his father's habits and mannerisms.

Rip Van Winkle, however, was one of those happy mortals, of foolish, well-oiled dispositions, who take the world as it comes, eat white bread or brown, whichever can be got with least thought or trouble, and would rather starve on a penny than work for a pound. If left to himself, he would have whistled life away in perfect contentment; but his wife kept on endlessly about his idleness, his carelessness, and the ruin he was bringing on his family. Morning, noon, and night, her tongue was constantly nagging. Rip had but one way of replying to all lectures of the kind, and that, by frequent use, had grown into a habit. He shrugged his shoulders, shook his head, rolled his eyes, but said nothing. This, however, always provoked a fresh rebuke from his wife; so that he was forced to leave the house to escape her tirades.

Rip's only support at home was his dog, Wolf, who was as much hen-pecked as his master; for Mrs. Van Winkle regarded them as companions in idleness, and even looked upon Wolf with an evil eye, as the cause of his master's going so often astray. Truth is, he was as courageous an animal as ever scoured the woods–but the moment Wolf entered the house his head fell and his tail drooped to the ground, or curled between his legs. At the least flourish of a broomstick or ladle, he would fly to the door with a yelp.

Poor Rip found his only alternative to escape from the labor of the farm and nagging of his wife, was to take gun in hand and stroll away into the woods. Here he would sometimes sit at the foot of a tree, and share the contents of his lunch with Wolf, with whom he sympathized as a fellow-sufferer in persecution.

In a long ramble on a fine autumn day, Rip had scrambled to one of the highest parts of the Kaatskill mountains. He was after his favorite sport of squirrel shooting, and the still solitudes had echoed and re-echoed with the reports of his gun. Panting and fatigued, he threw himself, late in the afternoon, on a knoll covered with mountain greenery that crowned the brow of a precipice. From an opening between the trees he could overlook all the lower country for many a mile of rich woodland. He saw at a distance the Hudson River, far, far below him, moving on its silent but majestic course, with the reflection of a purple cloud, or the sail of a lagging bark, here and there sleeping on its glassy bosom, and at last losing itself in the blue highlands.

On the other side he looked down into a deep mountain glen, wild, lonely, and shagged, the bottom filled with fragments from the impending cliffs, and scarcely lighted by the reflected rays of the setting sun. For some time Rip lay watching this scene. Evening was gradually advancing and the mountains began to throw their long blue shadows over the valleys. He saw that it would be dark long before he could reach the village, and he sighed heavily when he thought of encountering Mrs. Van Winkle.

As he was about to descend, he heard a voice from a distance, hallooing, "Rip Van Winkle! Rip Van Winkle!" He looked round, but could see nothing but a crow winging its solitary flight across the mountain. He thought his fancy must have deceived him, and turned again to descend, when he heard the same cry ring through the still evening air: "Rip Van Winkle! Rip Van Winkle!"–at the same time Wolf bristled up his back, and giving a low growl, skulked to his master's side, looking fearfully down into the glen. Rip now felt a vague apprehension stealing over him; he looked anxiously in the same direction, and perceived a strange figure slowly toiling up the rocks, and bending under the weight of something he carried on his back. He was surprised to see any human being in this lonely and unfrequented place, but supposing it to be someone of the neighborhood in need of his assistance, he hastened down to meet the mysterious man.

As Rip drew nearer, he was still more surprised by the stranger's appearance. He was a short square-built old fellow, with thick bushy hair, and a grizzled beard. His dress was of the antique Dutch fashion–a cloth jerkin strapped round the waist–several pair of breeches, decorated with rows of buttons down the sides, and bunches at the knees. He bore on his shoulder a stout keg, that seemed full of liquor, and made signs for Rip to approach and assist him with the load. Though rather shy and distrustful of this new acquaintance, Rip complied with his usual alacrity; and helping one another, they clambered up a narrow gully, apparently the dry bed of a mountain torrent. As they ascended, Rip every now and then heard long rolling peals, like distant thunder, that seemed to issue out of a deep ravine, or rather cleft, between lofty rocks, toward which their rugged path conducted. He paused for an instant, but supposing it to be the muttering of one of those thunderstorms that often take place in mountain heights, he continued on. Passing through the ravine, they came to a hollow, like a small amphitheatre, surrounded by perpendicular precipices, over the brinks of which impending trees shot their branches. During the whole time Rip and his companion had labored on in silence; for though Rip wondered what could be the object of carrying a keg of liquor up this wild mountain, yet there was something strange and incomprehensible about the unknown that inspired awe and checked familiarity.

On entering the amphitheatre, new objects of wonder presented themselves. On a level spot in the center was a group of odd-looking people bowling. They were dressed in a quaint outlandish fashion; some wore short doublets, others jerkins, with long knives in their belts, and most of them had enormous breeches, of similar style with that of the guide's. Their faces, too, were peculiar: one had a large beard, broad face, and small piggish eyes; another seemed to consist entirely of his nose, and wore a white sugar-loaf hat set off with a little red cock's tail. They all had beards of various shapes and colors. There was one who seemed to be the commander. He was a stout old gentleman, with a weather-beaten countenance; he wore a laced doublet, broad belt and hanger, high-crowned hat and feather, red stockings, and high-heeled shoes, with roses in them. The whole group reminded Rip of the figures in an old Flemish painting, in the parlor of Dominie Van Shaick, the village parson, which had been brought over from Holland at the time of the settlement.

What seemed particularly odd to Rip was, that though these folks were evidently amusing themselves, yet they maintained the gravest faces and the most mysterious silence. Without a doubt this was the most melancholy party of pleasure he had ever witnessed. Nothing interrupted the stillness of the scene but the noise of the balls, which, whenever they were rolled, echoed along the mountains like rumbling peals of thunder.

As Rip and his companion approached them, they suddenly desisted from their play, and stared at him with such fixed statue-like gazes and such strange expressions, that his heart turned within him, and his knees knocked together. His companion now emptied the contents of the keg into large flagons, and made signs to him to wait upon the company. He obeyed with fear and trembling; they quaffed the liquor in profound silence, and then returned to their game.

By degrees Rip's awe and apprehension subsided. He even ventured, when no eye was fixed upon him, to taste the beverage, which he found had much of the flavor of excellent beer. He was naturally a thirsty soul, and was soon tempted to have another glass. One taste provoked another; and he reiterated his visits to the keg so often that at length his senses were overpowered, his eyes swam in his head, his head gradually drooped forward, and he fell into a deep sleep.

On waking, he found himself on the green knoll where he had first seen the old man of the glen. He rubbed his eyes–it was a bright sunny morning. The birds were hopping and twittering among the bushes, and the eagle was wheeling aloft, and breasting the pure mountain breeze. "Surely," thought Rip, "I have not slept here all night." He recalled the occurrences before he fell asleep. The strange man with a keg of liquor–the mountain ravine–the wild retreat among the rocks–the strange party at ninepins–the flagon–*Oh! that keg! That wicked keg!* thought Rip. *What excuse shall I make to Mrs. Van Winkle?*

He looked round for his gun, but in place of the clean well-oiled shotgun, he found an old firelock lying by him, the barrel encrusted with rust, the lock falling off, and the stock worm-eaten. He now suspected that the grave men of the mountain had put a trick upon him, and having dosed him with liquor, had robbed him of his gun. Wolf, too, had disappeared, but he might have strayed away after a squirrel or partridge. He whistled after him and shouted his name, but all in vain; the echoes repeated his whistle and shout, but no dog was to be seen.

He determined to revisit the scene of the strange gathering, and if he met with any of the party, to demand his dog and gun. As he rose to walk, he found himself stiff in the joints. With some difficulty he got down into the glen where he found the gully up which he and his companion had ascended the preceding evening; but to his astonishment a mountain stream was now foaming down it, leaping from rock to rock, and filling the glen with babbling murmurs. He scrambled up its sides, working his way through thickets of birch, sassafras, and witch-hazel.

At length he reached the place where the ravine had opened through the cliffs to the amphitheatre; but no traces of such opening remained. The rocks presented a high impenetrable wall over which the torrent came tumbling in a sheet of feathery foam, and fell into a broad deep basin, black from the shadows of the surrounding forest. Here, then, poor Rip was brought to a stop. He again called and whistled for his dog, but he was only answered by the cawing of a flock of idle crows flying high in the air about a dry tree. What was to be done? The morning was passing away, and Rip felt famished for his breakfast. He grieved to lose his dog and gun; he dreaded to meet his wife; but it would not do to starve in the mountains. He shook his head, shouldered the rusty firelock, and, with a heart full of trouble and anxiety, turned homeward.

As he approached the village he met a number of people, but none whom he knew, which somewhat surprised him, for he had thought himself acquainted with everyone in the area. Their dress, too, was of a different fashion from that to which he was accustomed. They all stared at him with equal surprise, and whenever they looked at him, they invariably stroked their chins. The constant recurrence of this gesture induced Rip, involuntarily, to do the same, when to his astonishment, he found his beard had grown a foot long!

He had now entered the outskirts of the village. A troop of strange children ran at his heels, hooting after him, and pointing at his gray beard. The dogs, too, not one of which he recognized, barked at him as he passed. The very village was altered; it was larger and more populous. There were rows of houses that he had never seen before, and those that had been his familiar haunts had disappeared. Strange names were over the doors–strange faces at the windows–everything was strange. Confused and bewildered, he began to doubt whether both he and the world around him were not bewitched. Surely this was his native village, which he had left but the day before. There stood the Kaatskill mountains–there ran the silver Hudson at a distance–there was every hill and dale precisely as it had always been–Rip was sorely perplexed–"That flagon last night," thought he, "has addled my poor head sadly!"

It was with some difficulty that he found the way to his own house, which he approached with silent awe, expecting every moment to hear the shrill voice of Mrs. Van Winkle. He found the house gone to decay–the roof fallen in, the windows shattered, and the doors off the hinges. A half-starved dog that looked like Wolf was skulking about it. Rip called him by name, but the cur snarled, showed his teeth, and passed on. This was an unkind cut indeed–"My own dog," sighed poor Rip, "has forgotten me!"

He entered the house, which, to tell the truth, Mrs. Van Winkle had always kept in neat order. It was empty, forlorn, and apparently abandoned. This overcame all his hesitation–he called loudly for his wife and children–the lonely chambers rang for a moment with his voice, and then everything was silent.

He now hurried forth, and hastened to the village inn–but it too was gone. A large rickety wooden building stood in its place, with great gaping windows, some of them broken and mended with old hats and petticoats, and over the door was painted, "The Union Hotel, by Jonathan Doolittle." Instead of the great tree that used to shelter the quiet little Dutch inn, there now was a tall naked pole, with something on the top that looked like a red night-cap, and from it waved a flag, on which was an odd pattern of stars and stripes–all this was strange and incomprehensible. He recognized on the sign, however, the ruby face of King George, under which he had smoked so many a peaceful pipe; but even this was singularly metamorphosed. The red coat was changed for one of blue and buff, the head was decorated with a cocked hat, and underneath was painted in large characters, GENERAL WASHINGTON.

There was, as usual, a crowd of folk about the door, but none that Rip remembered. The very character of the people seemed changed. There was a busy, bustling, disputatious tone about it, instead of the accustomed drowsy tranquility. He looked in vain for the sage Nicholas Vedder, with his broad face, double chin, and fair long pipe, uttering clouds of tobacco-smoke instead of idle speeches; or Van Bummel, the schoolmaster, doling forth the contents of an ancient newspaper. In place of these, a lean, sour looking fellow, with his pockets full of handbills, was arguing about rights of citizens–elections–members of congress–liberty–Bunker's Hill–heroes of seventy-six–and other words, which were a perfect Babylonish jargon to the bewildered Van Winkle.

The appearance of Rip, with his long grizzled beard, his rusty shotgun, his odd clothes, and an army of women and children at his heels, soon attracted the attention of the tavern politicians. They crowded round him, eyeing him from head to foot with great curiosity. The speaker bustled up to him, and pulling him aside, inquired "on which side he voted?" Rip stared in vacant stupidity. Another short but busy little fellow pulled him by the arm, and, rising on tiptoe, inquired in his ear, "Whether he was Federal or Democrat?" Rip was equally at a loss to comprehend the question; when a knowing, self-important old gentleman, in a sharp cocked hat, made his way through the crowd, putting them to the right and left with his elbows as he passed, and planting himself before Van Winkle, demanded in an austere tone, "what brought him to the election with a gun on his shoulder, and a mob at his heels, and whether he meant to breed a riot in the village?"

"Alas! Gentlemen," cried Rip, somewhat dismayed, "I am a poor quiet man, a native of the place, and a loyal subject of the king, God bless him!"

Here a general shout burst from the bystanders–"A Tory! A Tory! A spy! A refugee!" It was with great difficulty that the self-important man in the cocked hat restored order; and, having assumed a most serious expression, demanded again to know what he came there for, and whom was he seeking? The poor man humbly assured him that he meant no harm, but merely came there in search of some of his neighbors, who used to spend time at the tavern.

"Well–who are they?–name them."

Rip thought for a moment, and inquired, "Where's Nicholas Vedder?"

There was a silence for a little while, when an old man replied, in a thin piping voice, "Nicholas Vedder! Why, he is dead and gone these eighteen years! There was a wooden tombstone in the churchyard that used to tell all about him, but that's rotten and gone too."

"Where's Brom Dutcher?"

"Oh, he went off to the army in the beginning of the war; some say he was killed at the storming of Stony Point–others say he was drowned in a squall at the foot of Antony's Nose. I don't know–he never came back again."

"Where's Van Bummel, the schoolmaster?"

"He went off to the wars too, was a great militia general, and is now in congress."

Rip's heart died away at hearing of these sad changes in his home and friends, and finding himself thus alone in the world. Every answer puzzled him too, by suggesting such enormous lapses of time, and of matters which he could not understand: war–congress–Stony Point–he had no courage to ask after any more friends, but cried out in despair, "Does nobody here know Rip Van Winkle?"

"Oh, Rip Van Winkle!" exclaimed two or three, "Oh, to be sure! That's Rip Van Winkle yonder, leaning against the tree."

Rip looked, and beheld a precise copy of himself, as he had gone up the mountain: apparently as lazy, and certainly as ragged. The poor fellow was now completely confounded. He doubted his own identity, and whether he was himself or another man. In the midst of his bewilderment, the man in the cocked hat demanded who he was, and what was his name?

"God knows," exclaimed he, at his wit's end. "I'm not myself–I'm somebody else–that's me yonder–no–that's somebody else got into my shoes–I was myself last night, but I fell asleep on the mountain, and they've changed my gun, and every thing's changed, and I'm changed, and I can't tell what's my name, or who I am!"

The bystanders now began to look at each other, nod, wink significantly, and tap their fingers against their foreheads. There was a whisper also, about securing the gun, and keeping the old fellow from doing mischief. At this critical moment a pretty young woman pressed through the throng to get a peep at the gray-bearded man. She had a chubby child in her arms, which, frightened at his looks, began to cry. "Hush, Rip," cried she, "hush, you little fool; the old man won't hurt you." The name of the child, the air of the mother, the tone of her voice, all awakened a series of memories in his mind. "What is your name, my good woman?" asked he.

"Judith Gardenier."

"And your father's name?"

"Ah, poor man, Rip Van Winkle was his name, but it's twenty years since he went away from home with his gun, and never has been heard of since–his dog came home without him; but whether he shot himself, or was carried away by the Indians, nobody can tell. I was only a little girl at the time."

Rip had but one question more to ask; but he put it with a faltering voice:

"Where's your mother?"

"Oh, she too died but a short time since–she broke a blood-vessel in a fit of passion at a peddler."

There was a drop of comfort, at least, in this intelligence. The honest man could contain himself no longer. He caught his daughter and her child in his arms. "I am your father!" cried he–"Young Rip Van Winkle once–old Rip Van Winkle now!–Does nobody know poor Rip Van Winkle?"

All stood amazed, until an old woman, tottering out from among the crowd, put her hand to her brow, and peering under it in his face for a moment, exclaimed, "Sure enough! It *is* Rip Van Winkle! Welcome home again, old neighbor–Why, where have you been these twenty long years?"

Rip's story was soon told, for the whole twenty years had been to him but one night. The neighbors stared when they heard it; some were seen to wink at each other, and the self-important man in the cocked hat, who, when the alarm was over, had returned to the field, screwed down the corners of his mouth, and shook his head–upon which there was a general shaking of the heads throughout the assemblage.

To make a long story short, the company broke up, and returned to the more important concerns of the election. Rip's daughter took him home to live with her; she had a snug, well-furnished house, and a stout cheery farmer for a husband, whom Rip remembered as one of the children that used to climb upon his back. As to Rip's son and heir, who was the very image of himself, he was hired to work on the farm, but gave in to his genetic disposition to attend to anything else but his business.

Rip now resumed his old walks and habits; he soon found many of his former cronies, though all rather the worse for the wear and tear of time; and preferred making friends among the younger generation, with whom he soon became very popular. Having nothing to do at home, and having arrived at that happy age when a man can be idle without disgrace, he took his place once more on the bench at the inn door, and was revered as one of the patriarchs of the village, and a chronicle of the old times "before the war."

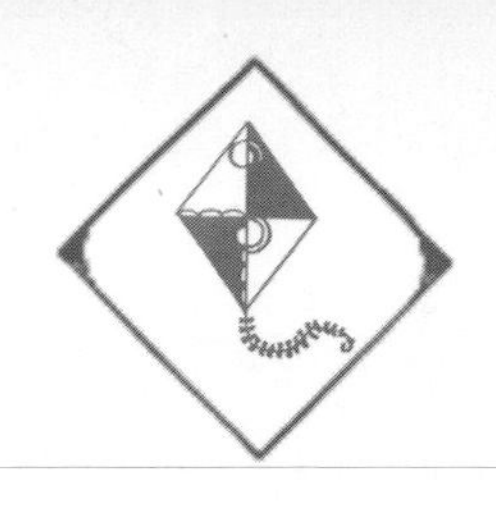

ELDORADO

EDGAR ALLAN POE

Gaily bedlight,
A gallant knight,
In sunshine and in shadow,
Had journeyed long,
Singing a song,
In search of Eldorado.

But he grew old–
This knight so bold–
And o'er his heart a shadow
Fell as he found
No spot of ground
That looked like Eldorado.

And, as his strength
Failed him at length,
He met a pilgrim shadow:
"Shadow," said he,

"Where can it be,
This land of Eldorado?"
"Over the mountains
Of the Moon,
Down the valley of the Shadow,
Ride, boldly ride,"
The shade replied,
"If you seek for Eldorado."

Two Old Men

Edward Lear

There was an Old Man with a beard,
Who said, "It is just as I feared!–
Two Owls and a Hen,
Four Larks and a Wren,
Have all built their nests in my beard!"

There was an Old Man who forgot,
That his tea was excessively hot.
When they said, "Let it cool,"
He answered, "You fool!
I shall pour it back into the pot."

M
M

CASEY AT THE BAT

ERNEST LAWRENCE THAYER

The outlook wasn't brilliant for the Mudville nine that day;
The score stood four to two with but one inning more to play.
And then when Cooney died at first, and Barrows did the same,
A sickly silence fell upon the patrons of the game.

A straggling few got up to go in deep despair. The rest
Clung to that hope which springs eternal in the human breast;
They thought if only Casey could get a whack at that–
We'd put up even money now with Casey at the bat.

But Flynn preceded Casey, as did also Jimmy Blake,
And the former was a lulu and the latter was a cake;
So upon that stricken multitude grim melancholy sat,
For there seemed but little chance of Casey's getting to the bat.

But Flynn let drive a single, to the wonderment of all,
And Blake, the much despised, tore the cover off the ball;

And when the dust had lifted, and the men saw what had occurred,
There was Jimmy safe at second and Flynn a-hugging third.

Then from five thousand throats and more there rose a lusty yell;
It rumbled through the valley, it rattled in the dell;
It knocked upon the mountain and recoiled upon the flat,
For Casey, mighty Casey, was advancing to the bat.

There was ease in Casey's manner as he stepped into his place;
There was pride in Casey's bearing and a smile on Casey's face.
And when, responding to the cheers, he lightly doffed his hat,
No stranger in the crowd could doubt 'twas Casey at the bat.

Ten thousand eyes were on him as he rubbed his hands with dirt;
Five thousand tongues applauded when he wiped them on his shirt.
Then while the writhing pitcher ground the ball into his hip,
Defiance gleamed in Casey's eye, a sneer curled Casey's lip.

And now the leather-covered sphere came hurtling through the air,
And Casey stood a-watching it in haughty grandeur there.
Close by the sturdy batsman the ball unheeded sped–
"That ain't my style," said Casey. "Strike one," the umpire said.

From the benches, black with people, there went up a muffled roar,
Like the beating of the storm waves on a stem and distant shore.

"Kill him! Kill the umpire!" shouted someone on the sand;
And it's likely they'd have killed him had not Casey raised his hand.

With a smile of Christian charity great Casey's visage shone;
He stilled the rising tumult; he bade the game go on;
He signaled to the pitcher, and once more the spheroid flew;
But Casey still ignored it, and the umpire said, "Strike two."

"Fraud!" cried the maddened thousands, and echo answered fraud;
But one scornful look from Casey and the audience was awed.
They saw his face grow stem and cold, they saw his muscles strain,
And they knew that Casey wouldn't let that ball go by again.

The sneer is gone from Casey's lip, his teeth are clenched in hate;
He pounds with cruel violence his bat upon the plate.
And now the pitcher holds the ball, and now he let's it go,
And now the air is shattered by the force of Casey's blow.

Oh, somewhere in this favored land the sun is shining bright;
The band is playing somewhere, and somewhere hearts are light,
And somewhere men are laughing, and somewhere children shout;
But there is no joy in Mudville–mighty Casey has struck out.

THE JOKE'S ON . . . WHO?

A tall ninth grader was acting up in class.

His teacher looked at him and said, "Act your age, not your shoe size."

The boy looks down at his size 14 shoes, then says, "But they're the same."

How do you catch a unique rabbit?

Unique up on it.

How do you catch a tame rabbit?

Tame way.

There once was a monster called Fred,
Who used to eat garlic in bed;
His mother said, "Son,
That's not really done,
Why don't you eat people instead?"

CHEATIN' JOE

One day in class, Mr. Johnson pulled Joe over to his desk after a test, and said, "Joe, I have a feeling that you have been cheating on your tests."

Joe was astounded and asked Mr. Johnson to prove it. "Well," said Mr. Johnson, "I was looking over your test and the question was, 'Who was our first president?' and the little girl that sits next to you, Mary, put 'George Washington,' and so did you."

"So, everyone knows that he was the first president."

"That may be," said Mr. Johnson. "But the next question was, 'Who freed the slaves?' Mary put Abraham Lincoln and so did you."

"Well, I read the history book last night and I remembered that," said Joe.

"Wait, wait," said Mr. Johnson. The next question was, 'Who was president during the Louisiana Purchase?' Mary put 'I don't know,' and you put, 'Me neither.'"

Why did the kid throw the clock out the window?

He wanted to see time fly.

The Zookeeper and Three Brothers

A zookeeper walked up to three brothers standing outside the lions' cage and asked them their names and what they were doing.

The first brother says, "My name's Tommy and I was trying to feed peanuts to the lions."

The second brother says, "My name's Billy and I was trying to feed peanuts to the lions."

The third brother says, "My name is Peanuts."

Grandpa: When I was your age I could name all of the presidents in the right order.

Smart Alec: Well sure . . . when you were my age there were only six of them.

A Goldfish Funeral

Young Bobby was in the backyard filling in a big hole when his neighbor peered over the fence.

Interested in what the precocious youngster was up to, he politely asked, "What are you up to there, Bobby?"

"My goldfish died," replied Bobby tearfully, without looking up, "and I've just buried him."

The neighbor looked puzzled, "That's an awfully big hole for just a goldfish, isn't it?"

Bobby stamped down the last heap of earth then replied, "That's because he's inside your stupid cat."

A Healthy Diet for Monsters

Did you hear about the snooker-mad monster? He went to the doctor because he didn't feel well. "What do you cat?" askcd thc doctor.

"For breakfast I usually have a couple of red snooker balls, and at lunchtime I eat a black, a pink, and two yellows. I have a brown with my tea in the afternoon, and then a blue and another pink for dinner."

"I know why you arc not fccling well," exclaimed the doctor. "You're not getting enough greens."

Why did the racecar driver keep making so many pit stops?

He kept asking for directions.

The Golden Goose

Jacob and Wilhelm Grimm

There was a man who had three sons, the youngest of whom was called Dummling, and was despised, mocked, and put down on every occasion.

It happened that the eldest wanted to go into the forest to hew wood, and before he went his mother gave him a beautiful sweet cake and a bottle of wine in order that he might not suffer from hunger or thirst.

When he entered the forest, he came upon a little gray-haired old man who bade him good-day, and said, "Do give me a piece of cake out of your pocket, and let me have a draught of your wine; I am so hungry and thirsty." But the prudent youth answered, "If I give you my cake and wine, I shall have none for myself; be off with you," and he left the little man standing and went on.

But when he began to hew down a tree, it was not long before he made a false stroke, and the axe cut him in the arm, so that he had to go home and have it bound up. And this was the little gray man's doing.

After this the second son went into the forest, and his mother gave him, like the eldest, a cake and a bottle of wine. The little old gray man met him likewise, and asked him for a piece of cake and a drink of wine. But the second son, too, said with much reason, "What I give you will be taken away from myself; be off!" and he left the little man standing and went on. His punishment, however, was not delayed; when he had made a few strokes at the tree he struck himself in the leg, so that he had to be carried home.

Then Dummling said, "Father, do let me go and cut wood." The father answered, "Your brothers have hurt themselves with it, leave it alone, you do not understand anything about it." But Dummling begged so long that at last he said, "Just go then, you will get wiser by hurting yourself." His mother gave him a cake made with water and baked in the cinders, and with it a bottle of sour beer.

When he came to the forest the little old gray man met him likewise, and greeting him, said, "Give me a piece of your cake and a drink out of your bottle; I am so hungry and thirsty." Dummling answered, "I have only cinder-cake and sour beer; if that pleases you, we will sit down and eat." So they sat down, and when Dummling pulled out his cinder-cake, it was a fine sweet cake, and the sour beer had become good wine. So they ate and drank, and after that the little man said, "Since you have a good heart, and are willing to divide what you have, I will give you good luck. There stands an old tree; cut it down, and you will find something at the roots." Then the old man took leave of him.

Dummling went and cut down the tree, and when it fell there was a goose sitting in the roots with feathers of pure gold. He lifted her up, and taking her with him, went to an inn where he thought he would stay the night. Now the host had three daughters, who saw the goose and were curious to know what such a wonderful bird might be, and would have liked to have one of its golden feathers.

The eldest thought, "I shall soon find an opportunity of pulling out a feather," and as soon as Dummling had gone out she seized the goose by the wing, but her fingers and hand remained sticking fast to it.

The second came soon afterwards, thinking only of how she might get a feather for herself, but she had scarcely touched her sister when she too was held fast.

At last the third also came with similar intent, and the others screamed out, "Keep away; for goodness' sake keep away!" But she did not understand why she was to keep away. "The others are there," she thought, "I may as well be there too," and ran to them; but as soon as she had touched her sister she remained sticking fast to her. So they had to spend the night with the goose.

The next morning Dummling took the goose under his arm and set out, without troubling himself about the three girls who were hanging to it. They were obliged to run after him continually, now left, now right, just as he was inclined to go.

In the middle of the fields the parson met them, and, when he saw the procession, he said, "For shame, you good-for-nothing girls, why are you running across the fields after this young man? Is that seemly?" At the same time he seized the youngest by the hand in order to pull her away, but as soon as he touched her he likewise stuck fast, and was himself obliged to run behind.

Before long the sexton came by and saw his master, the parson, running on foot behind three girls. He was astonished at this and called out, "Hi! your reverence, where are you going so quickly? Do not forget that we have a christening today!" and running after him he took him by the sleeve, but was also held fast to it.

While the five were trotting thus one behind the other, two laborers came with their hoes from the fields; the parson called out to them and begged that they would set him and the sexton free. But they had scarcely touched the sexton when they were held fast, and now there were seven of them running behind Dummling and the goose.

Soon afterwards he came to a city, where a king ruled who had a daughter who was so serious that no one could make her laugh. So he had put forth a decree that whosoever should be able to make her laugh should marry her. When Dummling heard this, he went with his goose and all her train before the King's daughter, and as soon as she saw the seven people running on and on, one behind the other, she began to laugh quite loudly, and as if she would never leave off. Thereupon Dummling asked to have her for his wife, and the wedding was celebrated. After the King's death Dummling inherited the kingdom, and lived a long time contentedly with his wife.

Minnie and Winnie

Alfred Tennyson

Minnie and Winnie
Slept in a shell.
Sleep, little ladies!
And they slept well.

Pink was the shell within,
Silver without;
Sounds of the great sea
Wandered about.

Sleep, little ladies,
Wake not soon!
Echo on echo
Dies to the moon.

Two bright stars
Peeped into the shell.

"What are they dreaming of?
Who can tell?"

Started a green linnet
Out of the croft;
Wake, little ladies,
The sun is aloft!

To A Butterfly

William Wordsworth

I've watched you now a full half hour
Self-poised upon that yellow flower;
And, little butterfly, indeed,
I know not if you sleep or feed.

How motionless!–not frozen seas
More motionless; and then,
What joy awaits you when the breeze
Hath found you out among the trees,
And calls you forth again!

This plot of orchard ground is ours,
My trees they are, my sister's flowers;
Here rest your wings when they are weary,
Here lodge as in a sanctuary!

Come to us often, fear no wrong,
Sit near us on the bough!
We'll talk of sunshine and of song,
And summer days when we were young;
Sweet childish days that were as long
As twenty days are now.

Playing Pilgrims

From *Little Women*

Louisa May Alcott

"Christmas won't be Christmas without any presents," grumbled Jo, lying on the rug.

"It's so dreadful to be poor!" sighed Meg, looking down at her old dress.

"I don't think it's fair for some girls to have plenty of pretty things, and other girls nothing at all," added little Amy, with an injured sniff.

"We've got Father and Mother, and each other," said Beth contentedly from her corner.

The four young faces on which the firelight shone brightened at the cheerful words, but darkened again as Jo said sadly, "We haven't got Father, and shall not have him for a long time." She didn't say "perhaps never," but each silently added it, thinking of Father far away, where the fighting was.

Nobody spoke for a minute; then Meg said in an altered tone, "You know the reason Mother proposed not having any presents this Christmas was because it is going to be a hard winter for everyone; and she thinks we ought not to spend money for pleasure, when our men are suffering so in the army. We can't do much, but we can make our little sacrifices, and ought to do it gladly. But I am afraid I don't." And Meg shook her head, as she thought regretfully of all the pretty things she wanted.

"But I don't think the little we should spend would do any good. We've each got a dollar, and the army wouldn't be much helped by our giving that. I agree not to expect anything from Mother or you, but I do want to buy *Undine and Sintram* for myself. I've wanted it *so* long," said Jo, who was a bookworm.

"I planned to spend mine in new music," said Beth, with a little sigh, which no one heard but the hearth brush and kettle holder.

"I shall get a nice box of Faber's drawing pencils. I really need them," said Amy decidedly.

"Mother didn't say anything about our money, and she won't wish us to give up everything. Let's each buy what we want, and have a little fun. I'm sure we work hard enough to earn it," cried Jo, examining the heels of her shoes in a gentlemanly manner.

"I know *I* do–teaching those tiresome children nearly all day, when I'm longing to enjoy myself at home," began Meg, in the complaining tone again.

"You don't have half such a hard time as I do," said Jo. "How would you like to be shut up for hours with a nervous, fussy old lady, who keeps you trotting, is never satisfied, and worries you till you you're ready to fly out the window or cry?"

"It's naughty to fret, but I do think washing dishes and keeping things tidy is the worst work in the world. It makes me cross, and my hands get so stiff, I can't practice well at all." And Beth looked at her rough hands with a sigh that any one could hear that time.

"I don't believe any of you suffer as I do," cried Amy, "for you don't have to go to school with impertinent girls, who plague you if you don't know your lessons, and laugh at your dresses, and label your father if he isn't rich, and insult you when your nose isn't nice."

"If you mean *libel,* I'd say so, and not talk about *labels,* as if Papa was a pickle bottle," advised Jo, laughing.

"I know what I mean, and you needn't be *statirical* about it. It's proper to use good words, and improve your *vocabilary,*" returned Amy, with dignity.

"Don't peck at one another, children. Don't you wish we had the money Papa lost when we were little, Jo? Dear me! How happy and good we'd be, if we had no worries!" said Meg, who could remember better times.

"You said the other day you thought we were a deal happier than the King children, for they were fighting and fretting all the time, in spite of their money."

"So I did, Beth. Well, I think we are. For though we do have to work, we make fun of ourselves, and are a pretty jolly set, as Jo would say."

"Jo does use such slang words!" observed Amy, with a reproving look at the long figure stretched on the rug.

Jo immediately sat up, put her hands in her pockets, and began to whistle.

"Don't, Jo. It's so boyish!"

"That's why I do it."

"I detest rude, unladylike girls!"

"I hate affected, niminy-piminy chits!"

"'Birds in their little nests agree,'" sang Beth, the peacemaker, with such a funny face that both sharp voices softened to a laugh, and the "pecking" ended for that time.

"Really, girls, you are both to be blamed," said Meg, beginning to lecture in her elder-sisterly fashion. "You are old enough to leave off boyish tricks, and to behave better, Josephine. It didn't matter so much when you were a little girl, but now you are so tall, and turn up your hair, you should remember that you are a young lady."

"I'm not! And if turning up my hair makes me one, I'll wear it in two tails till I'm twenty," cried Jo, pulling off her net, and shaking down a chestnut mane. "I hate to think I've got to grow up, and be Miss March, and wear long gowns, and look as prim as a China Aster! It's bad enough to be a girl, anyway, when I like boy's games and work and manners! I can't get over my disappointment in not being a boy. And it's worse than ever now, for I'm dying to go and fight with Papa. And I can only stay home and knit, like a poky old woman!" And Jo shook the blue army sock till the needles rattled like castanets, and her ball bounded across the room.

"Poor Jo! It's too bad, but it can't be helped. So you must try to be contented with making your name boyish, and playing brother to us girls," said Beth, stroking the rough head with a hand that all the dish washing and dusting in the world could not make ungentle in its touch.

"As for you, Amy," continued Meg, "you are altogether too particular and prim. Your airs are funny now, but you'll grow up an affected little goose, if you don't take care. I like your nice manners and refined ways of speaking, when you don't try to be elegant. But your absurd words are as bad as Jo's slang."

"If Jo is a tomboy and Amy a goose, what am I, please?" asked Beth, ready to share the lecture.

"You're a dear, and nothing else," answered Meg warmly, and no one contradicted her, for the "Mouse" was the pet of the family.

As young readers like to know "how people look," we will take this moment to give them a little sketch of the four sisters, who sat knitting away in the twilight, while the December snow fell quietly without, and the fire crackled cheerfully within. It was a comfortable room, though the carpet was faded and the furniture very plain, for a good picture or two hung on the walls, books filled the recesses, chrysanthemums and Christmas roses bloomed in the windows, and a pleasant atmosphere of home peace pervaded it.

Margaret, the eldest of the four, was sixteen, and very pretty, being plump and fair, with large eyes, plenty of soft brown hair, a sweet mouth, and white hands, of which she was rather vain. Fifteen-year-old Jo was very tall, thin, and brown, and reminded one of a colt, for she never seemed to know what to do with her long limbs, which were very much in her way. She had a decided mouth, a comical nose, and sharp, gray eyes, which appeared to see everything, and were by turns fierce, funny, or thoughtful. Her long, thick hair was her one beauty, but it was usually bundled into a net, to be out of her way. Round shoulders had Jo, big hands and feet, a flyaway look to her clothes, and the uncomfortable appearance of a girl who was rapidly shooting up into a woman and didn't like it. Elizabeth–or Beth, as everyone called her–was a rosy, smooth-haired, bright-eyed girl of thirteen, with a shy manner, a timid voice, and a peaceful expression which was seldom disturbed. Her father called her "Little Miss Tranquility," and the name suited her excellently, for she seemed to live in a happy world of her own, only venturing out to meet the few whom she trusted and loved. Amy, though the youngest, was a most important person, in her own opinion at least. A regular snow maiden, with blue eyes, and yellow hair curling on her shoulders, pale and slender, and always carrying herself like a young lady mindful of her manners. What the characters of the four sisters were we will leave to be found out.

The clock struck six and, having swept up the hearth, Beth put a pair of slippers down to warm. Somehow the sight of the old shoes had a good effect upon the girls, for Mother was coming, and everyone brightened to welcome her. Meg stopped lecturing, and lighted the lamp, Amy got out of the easy chair without being asked, and Jo forgot how tired she was as she sat up to hold the slippers nearer to the blaze.

"They are quite worn out. Marmee must have a new pair."

"I thought I'd get her some with my dollar," said Beth.

"No, I shall!" cried Amy.

"I'm the oldest," began Meg, but Jo cut in with a decided, "I'm the man of the family now Papa is away, and I shall provide the slippers, for he told me to take special care of Mother while he was gone."

"I'll tell you what we'll do," said Beth, "let's each get her something for Christmas, and not get anything for ourselves."

"That's like you, dear! What will we get?" exclaimed Jo.

Everyone thought soberly for a minute, then Meg announced, as if the idea was suggested by the sight of her own pretty hands, "I shall give her a nice pair of gloves."

"Army shoes, best to be had," cried Jo.

"Some handkerchiefs, all hemmed," said Beth.

"I'll get a little bottle of cologne. She likes it, and it won't cost much, so I'll have some left to buy my pencils," added Amy.

"How will we give the things?" asked Meg.

"Put them on the table, and bring her in and see her open the bundles. Don't you remember how we used to do on our birthdays?" answered Jo.

"I used to be so frightened when it was my turn to sit in the chair with the crown on, and see you all come marching round to give the presents, with a kiss. I liked the things and the kisses, but it was dreadful to have you sit looking at me while I opened the bundles," said Beth, who was toasting her face and the bread for tea at the same time.

"Let Marmee think we are getting things for ourselves, and then surprise her. We must go shopping tomorrow afternoon, Meg. There is so much to do about the play for Christmas night," said Jo, marching up and down, with her hands behind her back, and her nose in the air.

"I don't mean to act any more after this time. I'm getting too old for such things," observed Meg, who was as much a child as ever about "dressing-up" frolics.

"You won't stop, I know, as long as you can trail round in a white gown with your hair down, and wear gold-paper jewelry. You are the best actress we've got, and there'll be an end of everything if you quit the boards," said Jo. "We ought to rehearse tonight. Come here, Amy, and do the fainting scene, for you are as stiff as a poker in that."

"I can't help it. I never saw anyone faint, and I don't choose to make myself all black and blue, tumbling flat as you do. If I can go down easily, I'll drop. If I can't, I shall fall into a chair and be graceful. I don't care if Hugo does come at me with a pistol," returned Amy, who was not gifted with dramatic power, but was chosen because she was small enough to be borne out shrieking by the villain of the piece.

"Do it this way. Clasp your hands so, and stagger across the room, crying frantically, 'Roderigo! Save me! Save me!'" and away went Jo, with a melodramatic scream which was truly thrilling.

Amy followed, but she poked her hands out stiffly before her, and jerked herself along as if she went by machinery, and her "Ow!" was more suggestive of pins being run into her than of fear and anguish. Jo gave a despairing groan, and Meg laughed outright, while Beth let her bread burn as she watched the fun with interest. "It's no use! Do the best you can when the time comes, and if the audience laughs, don't blame me. Come on, Meg."

Then things went smoothly, for Don Pedro defied the world in a speech of two pages without a single break. Hagar, the witch, chanted an awful incantation over her kettleful of simmering toads, with weird effect. Roderigo rent his chains asunder manfully, and Hugo died in agonies of remorse and arsenic, with a wild, "Ha! ha!"

"It's the best we've had yet," said Meg, as the dead villain sat up and rubbed his elbows.

"I don't see how you can write and act such splendid things, Jo. You're a regular Shakespeare!" exclaimed Beth, who firmly believed that her sisters were gifted with wonderful genius in all things.

"Not quite," replied Jo modestly. "I do think *The Witches Curse, An Operatic Tragedy* is rather a nice thing, but I'd like to try *Macbeth,* if we only had a trapdoor for Banquo. I always wanted to do the killing part. 'Is that a dagger that I see before me?'" muttered Jo, rolling her eyes and clutching at the air, as she had seen a famous tragedian do.

"No, it's the toasting fork, with Mother's shoe on it instead of the bread. Beth's stage-struck!" cried Meg, and the rehearsal ended in a general burst of laughter.

"Glad to find you so merry, my girls," said a cheery voice at the door, and actors and audience turned to welcome a tall, motherly lady with a "can I help you" look about her which was truly delightful. She was not elegantly dressed, but a noble-looking woman, and the girls thought the gray cloak and unfashionable bonnet covered the most splendid mother in the world.

"Well, dearies, how have you got on today? There was so much to do, getting the boxes ready to go tomorrow, that I didn't come home to dinner.

Has anyone called, Beth? How is your cold, Meg? Jo, you look tired to death. Come and kiss me, baby."

While making these maternal inquiries, Mrs. March got her wet things off, her warm slippers on, and sitting down in the easy chair, drew Amy to her lap, preparing to enjoy the happiest hour of her busy day. The girls flew about, trying to make things comfortable, each in her own way. Meg arranged the tea table, Jo brought wood and set chairs, dropping, overturning, and clattering everything she touched. Beth trotted to and fro between parlor kitchen, quiet and busy, while Amy gave directions to everyone, as she sat with her hands folded.

As they gathered about the table, Mrs. March said, with a particularly happy face, "I've got a treat for you after supper."

A quick, bright smile went round like a streak of sunshine. Beth clapped her hands, regardless of the biscuit she held, and Jo tossed up her napkin, crying, "A letter! A letter! Three cheers for Father!"

"Yes, a nice long letter. He is well, and thinks he shall get through the cold season better than we feared. He sends all sorts of loving wishes for Christmas, and an especial message to you girls," said Mrs. March, patting her pocket as if she had got a treasure there.

"Hurry and get done! Don't stop to quirk your little finger and simper over your plate, Amy," cried Jo, choking on her tea and dropping her bread, butter side down, on the carpet in her haste to get at the treat.

Beth ate no more, but crept away to sit in her shadowy corner and brood over the delight to come, till the others were ready.

"I think it was so splendid in Father to go as chaplain when he was too old to be drafted, and not strong enough for a soldier," said Meg warmly.

"Don't I wish I could go as a drummer, a *vivan*–what's its name? Or a nurse, so I could be near him and help him," exclaimed Jo, with a groan.

"It must be very disagreeable to sleep in a tent, and eat all sorts of bad-tasting things, and drink out of a tin mug," sighed Amy.

"When will he come home, Marmee?" asked Beth, with a little quiver in her voice.

"Not for many months, dear, unless he is sick. He will stay and do his work faithfully as long as he can, and we won't ask for him back a minute sooner than he can be spared. Now come and hear the letter."

They all drew to the fire, Mother in the big chair with Beth at her feet, Meg and Amy perched on either arm of the chair, and Jo leaning on the back, where no one would see any sign of emotion if the letter should happen to be touching. Very few letters were written in those hard times that were not touching, especially those which fathers sent home. In this one little was said of the hardships endured, the dangers faced, or the homesickness conquered. It was a cheerful, hopeful letter, full of lively descriptions of camp life, marches, and military news, and only at the end did the writer's heart overflow with fatherly love and longing for the little girls at home.

"Give them all of my dear love and a kiss. Tell them I think of them by day, pray for them by night, and find my best comfort in their affection at all times. A year seems very long to wait before I see them, but remind them that while we wait we may all work, so that these hard days need not be wasted. I know they will remember all I said to them, that they will be loving children to you, will do their duty faithfully, fight their bosom enemies bravely, and conquer themselves so beautifully that when I come back to them I may be fonder and prouder than ever of my little women." Everybody sniffed when they came to that part. Jo wasn't ashamed of the great tear that dropped off the end of her nose, and Amy never minded the rumpling of her curls as she hid her face on her mother's shoulder and sobbed out, "I *am* a selfish girl! But I'll truly try to be better, so he mayn't be disappointed in me by-and-by."

"We all will," cried Meg. "I think too much of my looks and hate to work, but won't any more, if I can help it."

"I'll try and be what he loves to call me, 'a little woman' and not be rough and wild, but do my duty here instead of wanting to be somewhere else," said Jo, thinking that keeping her temper at home was a much harder task than facing a rebel or two down South.

Beth said nothing, but wiped away her tears with the blue army sock and began to knit with all her might, losing no time in doing the duty that lay nearest her, while she resolved in her quiet little soul to be all that Father hoped to find her when the year brought round the happy coming home.

Mrs. March broke the silence that followed Jo's words by saying in her cheery voice, "Do you remember how you used to play Pilgrim's Progress when you were little things? Nothing delighted you more than to have me tie my piece bags on your backs for burdens, give you hats and sticks and rolls of paper, and let you travel through the house from the cellar, which was the City of Destruction, up, up, to the housetop, where you had all the lovely things you could collect to make a Celestial City."

"What fun it was, especially going by the lions, fighting Apollyon, and passing through the valley where the hobgoblins were," said Jo.

"I liked the place where the bundles fell off and tumbled downstairs," said Meg.

"I don't remember much about it, except that I was afraid of the cellar and the dark entry, and always liked the cake and milk we had up at the top. If I wasn't too old for such things, I'd rather like to play it over again," said Amy, who began to talk of renouncing childish things at the mature age of twelve.

"We never are too old for this, my dear, because it is a play we are playing all the time in one way or another. Our burdens are here, our road is before us, and the longing for goodness and happiness is the guide that leads us through many troubles and mistakes to the peace which is a true Celestial City. Now, my little pilgrims, suppose you begin again, not in play, but in earnest, and see how far on you can get before Father comes home."

"Really, Mother? Where are our bundles?" asked Amy, who was a very literal young lady.

"Each of you told what your burden was just now, except Beth. I rather think she hasn't got any," said her mother.

"Yes, I have. Mine is dishes and dusters, and envying girls with nice pianos, and being afraid of people."

Beth's bundle was such a funny one that everybody wanted to laugh, but nobody did, for it would have hurt her feelings very much.

"Let us do it," said Meg thoughtfully. "It is only another name for trying to be good, and the story may help us, for though we do want to be good, it's hard work and we forget, and don't do our best."

"We were in the Slough of Despond tonight, and Mother came and pulled us out as Help did in the book. We ought to have our roll of directions, like Christian. What shall we do about that?" asked Jo, delighted with the fancy which lent a little romance to the very dull task of doing her duty.

"Look under your pillows Christmas morning, and you will find your guidebook," replied Mrs. March.

They talked over the new plan while old Hannah cleared the table, then out came the four little work baskets, and the needles flew as the girls made sheets for Aunt March. It was uninteresting sewing, but tonight no one grumbled. They adopted Jo's plan of dividing the long seams into four parts, and calling the quarters Europe, Asia, Africa, and America, and in that way got on capitally, especially when they talked about the different countries as they stitched their way through them.

At nine they stopped work, and sang, as usual, before they went to bed. No one but Beth could get much music out of the old piano, but she had a way of softly touching the yellow keys and making a pleasant accompaniment to the simple songs they sang. Meg had a voice like a flute, and she and her mother led the little choir. Amy chirped like a cricket, and Jo wandered through the airs at her own sweet will, always coming out at the wrong place with a croak or a quaver that spoiled the most pensive tune. They had always done this from the time they could lisp, "Crinkle, crinkle, 'ittle 'tar," and it had become a household custom, for the mother was a born singer. The first sound in the morning was her voice as she went about the house singing like a lark, and the last sound at night was the same cheery sound, for the girls never grew too old for that familiar lullaby.

A MIDSUMMER-NIGHT'S DREAM

FROM *TALES FROM SHAKESPEARE*

CHARLES AND MARY LAMB

There was a law in the city of Athens that gave its citizens the power of forcing their daughters to marry whomsoever they pleased; for if a daughter refused to marry the man her father had chosen to be her husband, the father was empowered by this law to cause her to be put to death. But because fathers do not often desire the death of their own daughters, even though they do happen to prove a little obstinate, this law was seldom or never put in execution, though perhaps the young ladies of that city were not infrequently threatened by their parents with the terrors of it.

However, there was one instance of an old man named Egeus, who actually did come before Theseus (at that time the reigning duke of Athens), to complain that his daughter Hermia, whom he had commanded to marry Demetrius–a young man of a noble Athenian family–refused to obey him, because she loved another young Athenian, named Lysander. Egeus demanded justice of Theseus, and desired that this cruel law might be put into force against his daughter.

Hermia pleaded in excuse for her disobedience, that Demetrius had formerly professed love for her dear friend Helena, and that Helena loved Demetrius to distraction; but this honorable reason, which Hermia gave for not obeying her father's command, did not move the stern Egeus.

Theseus, though a great and merciful prince, had no power to alter the laws of his country; therefore he could only give Hermia four days to consider of it: and at the end of that time, if she still refused to marry Demetrius, she was to be put to death.

When Hermia was dismissed from the presence of the duke, she went to her lover Lysander, and told him the peril she was in, and that she must either give him up and marry Demetrius, or lose her life in four days.

Lysander was in great affliction at hearing these evil tidings; but recollecting that he had an aunt who lived at some distance from Athens, and the cruel law could not be put in force against Hermia there (this law not extending beyond the boundaries of the city), he proposed to Hermia that she should steal out of her father's house that night, and go with him to his aunt's house, where he would marry her. "I will meet you," said Lysander, "in the wood a few miles outside the city; in that delightful wood where we have so often walked with Helena in the pleasant month of May."

To this proposal Hermia joyfully agreed; and she told no one of her intended flight but her friend Helena. Helena (as maidens will sometimes do foolish things for love) very ungenerously resolved to go and tell this to Demetrius, though she could hope no benefit from betraying her friend's secret, but the poor pleasure of following her faithless lover to the wood; for she well knew that Demetrius would go after Hermia.

The wood in which Lysander and Hermia proposed to meet was the favorite haunt of those little beings known by the name of *Fairies*.

Oberon the king, and Titania the queen of the fairies, with all their tiny train of followers, in this wood held their midnight revels.

Between this little king and queen of sprites there happened, at this time, a sad disagreement; they never met by moonlight in the shady walks of this pleasant wood, but they were quarrelling, till all their fairy elves would creep into acorn-cups and hide themselves for fear.

The cause of this unhappy disagreement was Titania's refusing to give Oberon a little changeling boy, whose mother had been Titania's friend; and upon her death the fairy queen stole the child from its nurse, and brought him up in the woods.

The night on which the lovers were to meet in this wood, as Titania was walking with some of her maids of honor, she met Oberon attended by his train of fairy courtiers. "What an unfortunate meeting by moonlight, proud Titania," said the fairy king. The queen replied, "What, jealous Oberon, is it you? Fairies, hurry along–I have sworn to avoid his company."–"Tarry, rash fairy," said Oberon. "Am not I thy lord? Why does Titania cross her Oberon? Give me your little changeling boy to be my page."

"Set your heart at rest," answered the queen; "I would not sell the boy for your entire fairy kingdom." She then left her lord in great anger. "Well, go your way," said Oberon "before the morning dawns I will torment you for this insult."

Oberon then sent for Puck, his chief favorite and privy counselor. Puck (or as he was sometimes called, Robin Goodfellow) was a shrewd and knavish sprite that used to play comical pranks in the neighboring villages–sometimes getting into the dairies and skimming the milk, sometimes plunging his light and airy form into the butter-churn, and while he was dancing his fantastic shape in the churn, in vain the dairymaid would labor to change her cream into butter: nor had the village swains any better success; whenever Puck chose to play his tricks in the brewing copper, the ale was sure to be spoiled. When a few good neighbors met to drink some comfortable ale together, Puck would jump into the bowl of ale in the likeness of a roasted crab, and when some old goody was going to drink he would bob against her lips, and spill the ale over her withered chin; and presently after, when the same old dame was gravely seating herself to tell her neighbors a sad and melancholy story, Puck would slip her three-legged stool from under her, and down toppled the poor old woman, and then the old gossips would hold their sides and laugh at her, and swear they never wasted a merrier hour.

"Come hither, Puck," said Oberon to this little merry wanderer of the night; "fetch me the flower which maids call *Love in Idleness;* the juice of that little purple flower laid on the eyelids of those who sleep will make them, when they awake, dote on the first thing they see. Some of the juice of that flower I will drop on the eyelids of my Titania when she is asleep; and the first thing she looks upon when she opens her eyes she will fall in love with, even though it be a lion or a bear, a meddling monkey, or a busy ape; and before I will take this charm from off her sight, which I can do with another charm I know of, I will make her give me that boy to be my page."

Puck, who loved mischief of all kinds, was highly interested with this plan of his master, and ran to seek the flower; and while Oberon was waiting the return of Puck, he observed Demetrius and Helena enter the wood; he overheard Demetrius reproaching Helena for following him, and after many unkind words on his part, and gentle expostulations from Helena, reminding him of his former love and professions of true faith to her, he left her, as he said, to the mercy of the wild beasts, and she ran after him as swiftly as she could.

The fairy king, who was always friendly to true lovers, felt great compassion for Helena; and perhaps, as Lysander said they used to walk by moonlight in this pleasant wood, Oberon might have seen Helena in those happy times when she was beloved by Demetrius. However that might be, when Puck returned with the little purple flower, Oberon said to his favorite, "Take a part of this flower; there has been a sweet Athenian lady here, who is in love with a disdainful youth; if you find him sleeping, drop some of the love-juice in his eyes, but contrive to do it when she is near him, that the first thing he sees when he awakes may be this despised lady. You will know the man by the Athenian garments which he wears." Puck promised to manage this matter very dexterously: and then Oberon went, unperceived by Titania, to her bower, where she was preparing to go to rest. Her fairy bower was a bank, where wild thyme, cowslips, and sweet violets grew under a canopy of woodbine, musk-roses, and eglantine. There Titania always slept some part of the night; her coverlet the enameled skin of a snake, which, though a small mantle, was wide enough to wrap a fairy in.

He found Titania giving orders to her fairies, how they were to employ themselves while she slept. "Some of you," said her majesty, "must kill cankers in the musk-rose buds, and some wage war with the bats for their leathern wings, to make my small elves coats; and some of you keep watch that the clamorous owl, that nightly hoots, come not near me. But first sing me to sleep." Then they began to sing this song:

"You spotted snakes with double tongue,
Thorny hedgehogs, be not seen
Newts and blind-worms do no wrong
Come not near our Fairy Queen.
Philomel, with melody
Sing in our sweet lullaby
Lulla, lulla, lullaby; lulla, lulla, lullaby;
Never harm, nor spell, nor charm,
Come our lovely lady nigh;
So good night with lullaby."

When the fairies had sung their queen asleep with this pretty lullaby, they left her to perform the important services she had assigned them. Oberon then softly drew near his Titania, and dropped some of the love-juice on her eyelids, saying: "What thou seest when thou wake, do it for thy true-love take."

But returning to Hermia, she made her escape out of her father's house that night, to avoid the death she was doomed to for refusing to marry Demetrius. When she entered the wood, she found her dear Lysander waiting for her, to conduct her to his aunt's house; but before they had passed half through the wood, Hermia was so much fatigued, that Lysander, who was very careful of this dear lady, who had proved her affection for him even by hazarding her life for his sake, persuaded her to rest till morning on a bank of soft moss, and lying down himself on the ground at some little distance, they soon fell fast asleep. Here they were found by Puck, who, seeing a handsome young man asleep, and perceiving that his clothes were made in the Athenian fashion, and that a pretty lady was sleeping near him, concluded that this must be the Athenian maid and her disdainful lover whom Oberon had sent him to seek; and he naturally enough conjectured that, as they were alone together, she must be the first thing he would see when he awoke; so, without more ado, he proceeded to pour some of the juice of the little purple flower into his eyes. But as it happened, Helena passed by that way and instead of Hermia, *she* was the first object Lysander beheld when he opened his eyes; and strange to relate, so powerful was the love-charm, all his love for Hermia vanished away, and Lysander fell in love with Helena.

Had he first seen Hermia when he awoke, the blunder Puck committed would have been of no consequence, for he could not love that faithful lady too well; but for poor Lysander to be forced by a fairy love-charm to forget his own true Hermia, and to run after another lady, and leave Hermia asleep quite alone in a wood at midnight, was a sad chance indeed.

Thus this misfortune happened. Helena, as already mentioned, endeavored to keep pace with Demetrius when he ran away so rudely from her; but she could not keep up with him long, men being always better runners in a long race than ladies. Helena soon lost sight of Demetrius; and as she was wandering about, dejected and forlorn, she arrived at the place where Lysander was sleeping. "Ah!" said she, "this is Lysander lying on the ground: is he dead or asleep?" Then, gently touching him, she said: "Good sir, if you are alive, awake." Upon this Lysander opened his eyes, and (the love-charm beginning to work) immediately addressed her in terms of extravagant love and admiration; telling her she as much excelled Hermia in beauty as a dove does a raven, and that he would run through fire for her sweet sake; and many more such lover-like speeches. Helena, knowing Lysander was her friend Hermia's lover, and that he was solemnly engaged to marry her, was in the utmost rage when she heard herself addressed in this manner, for she thought (as well she might) that Lysander was making a jest of her. "Oh!" said she, "why was I born to be mocked and scorned by everyone? Is it not enough, is it not enough, young man, that I can never get a sweet look or a kind word from Demetrius; but you, sir, must pretend in this disdainful manner to court me? I thought, Lysander, you were a lord of more true gentleness." Saying these words in great anger, she ran away; and Lysander followed her, quite forgetful of his own Hermia, who was still asleep.

When Hermia awoke, she was quite frightened at finding herself alone. She wandered about the wood, not knowing what was become of Lysander, or which way to go to seek for him. In the meantime Demetrius, not being able to find Hermia and his rival Lysander, and fatigued with his fruitless search, was observed by Oberon fast asleep. Oberon had learnt by some questions he had asked of Puck, that he had applied the love-charm to the wrong person's eyes; and now having found the person first intended, he touched the eyelids of the sleeping Demetrius with the love-juice, and he instantly awoke; and the first thing he saw being Helena, he, as Lysander had done before, began to address love-speeches to her; and just at that moment Lysander made his appearance, followed by Hermia (for through Puck's unlucky mistake it was now become Hermia's turn to run after her lover) and then Lysander and Demetrius, both speaking together, professed their undying love for Helena, each being under the influence of the same potent charm.

The astonished Helena thought that Demetrius, Lysander, and her once dear friend Hermia, were all in a plot together to make a jest of her.

Hermia was as much surprised as Helena; she knew not why Lysander and Demetrius, who both before loved her, now loved Helena; and to Hermia the matter seemed to be no jest. The ladies, who before had always been the dearest of friends, now fell to high words together.

"Unkind Hermia," said Helena, "you have convinced Lysander to vex me with mock praises; and your other lover Demetrius–who has always rejected me–have you not asked him to call me Goddess, Nymph, rare, precious, and celestial? He would not speak this way to me, if you did not set him on to make a jest of me. Unkind Hermia, to join with men in scorning your poor friend. Have you forgot our school-day friendship? Hermia, it is not friendly, it is not maidenly to join with men in scorning your poor friend."

"I am amazed at your passionate words," said Hermia. "I scorn you not; it seems you scorn me."

"Aye, do," returned Helena, "persevere, counterfeit serious looks, and make mouths at me when I turn my back; then wink at each other, and continue your jest. If you had any pity, grace, or manners, you would not use me thus."

While Helena and Hermia were speaking these angry words to each other, Demetrius and Lysander left them, to fight together in the wood for the love of Helena. When the women found the gentlemen had left them, they departed, and once more wandered weary in the wood in search of their lovers.

As soon as they were gone, the fairy king, who with little Puck had been listening to their quarrels, said to him, "This is your negligence, Puck; or did you do this intentionally?"

"Believe me, king of shadows," answered Puck, "it was an honest mistake; did not you tell me I should know the man by his Athenian garments? However, I am not sorry this has happened, for I think their jangling is most amusing."

"You heard," said Oberon, "that Demetrius and Lysander are gone to seek a convenient place to fight in. I command you to overhang the night with a thick fog, and lead these quarrelsome lovers so astray in the dark, that they shall not be able to find each other. Counterfeit each of their voices to the other, and with bitter taunts provoke them to follow you, while they think it is their rival's tongue they hear. See you do this, till they are so weary they can go no farther; and when you find they are asleep, drop the juice of this other flower into Lysander's eyes, and when he awakes he will forget his new love for Helena, and return to his old passion for Hermia. Then the two fair ladies may each be happy with the man she loves, and they will think all that has passed is only an unpleasant dream. About this quickly, Puck, and I will go and see what sweet love my Titania has found."

Titania was still sleeping, and Oberon found a clown near her, who had lost his way in the wood and was also asleep. "This fellow," said he, "shall be my Titania's true love;" and clapping a donkey's head over the clown's, it seemed to fit him as well as if it had grown upon his own shoulders. Though Oberon fixed the donkey's head on very gently, it awakened him, and rising up, unconscious of what Oberon had done to him, he went towards the bower where the fairy queen slept.

"Ah! What angel do I see?" said Titania, opening her eyes, and the juice of the little purple flower beginning to take effect; "are you as wise as you are beautiful?"

"Why, mistress," said the foolish clown, "if I have wit enough to find the way out of this wood, I have enough to serve my turn."

"Out of the wood do not desire to go," said the enamored queen. "I am a spirit of no common rate. I love you. Go with me, and I will give you fairies to attend upon you." She then called four of her fairies: their names were, Pease-blossom, Cobweb, Moth, and Mustard-seed.

"Attend," said the queen, "upon this sweet gentleman; hop in his walks, and gambol in his sight; feed him with grapes and apricots, and steal for him the honey-bags from the bees. Come, sit with me," she said to the clown, "and let me play with your amiable hairy cheeks, my beautiful donkey, and kiss your fair large ears, my gentle joy!"

"Where is Pease-blossom?" said the donkey-headed clown, not much regarding the fairy queen's courtship, but very proud of his new attendants.

"Here, sir," said little Pease-blossom.

"Scratch my head," said the clown. "Where is Cobweb?"

"Here, sir," said Cobweb.

"Good Mr. Cobweb," said the foolish clown, "kill me the red bumble bee on the top of that thistle yonder; and, good Mr. Cobweb, bring me the honey-bag. Do not fret yourself too much in the action, Mr. Cobweb, and take care the honey-bag break not; I should be sorry to have you overflown with a honey-bag. Where is Mustard-seed?"

"Here, sir," said Mustard-seed: "what do you wish for?"

"Nothing," said the clown, "good Mr. Mustard-seed, but to help Mr. Pease-blossom to scratch; I must go to a barber's, Mr. Mustard-seed, for methinks I am marvelous hairy about the face."

"My sweet love," said the queen, "what will you have to eat? I have a venturous fairy shall seek the squirrel's hoard, and fetch you some new nuts."

"I had rather have a handful of dried peas," said the clown, who with his donkey's head had got an donkey's appetite. "But, I pray, let none of your people disturb me, for I have a mind to sleep."

"Sleep, then," said the queen, "and I will hold you in my arms. O how I love you! How I dote upon you!"

When the fairy king saw the clown sleeping in the arms of his queen, he advanced within her sight, and reproached her with having lavished her favors upon a donkey. This she could not deny, as the clown was then sleeping within her arms, with his donkey's head covered with flowers.

When Oberon had teased her for some time, he again demanded the changeling boy; which she, ashamed of being discovered by her lord with her new favorite, did not dare to refuse him.

Oberon, having now obtained the little boy he had so long wished for to be his page, took pity on the disgraceful situation into which, by his merry contrivance, he had brought his Titania and threw some of the juice of the other flower into her eyes; and the fairy queen immediately recovered her senses, and wondered at her late dotage, saying how she now loathed the sight of the strange monster.

Oberon likewise took the donkey's head off the clown, and left him to finish his nap with his own fool's head upon his shoulders.

Oberon and his Titania being now perfectly reconciled, he related to her the history of the lovers, and their midnight quarrels; and she agreed to go with him and see the end of their adventures.

The fairy king and queen found the lovers and their fair ladies, at no great distance from each other, sleeping on a grass-plot; for Puck, to make amends for his former mistake, had contrived with the utmost diligence to bring them all to the same spot, unknown to each other, and he had carefully removed the charm from off the eyes of Lysander with the antidote the fairy king gave to him.

Hermia awoke first, and finding her lost Lysander asleep so near her, was looking at him and wondering at his strange behavior. Lysander presently opening his eyes, and seeing his dear Hermia, recovered his reason which the fairy charm had before clouded, and also his love for Hermia. They began to talk over the adventures of the night, doubting if these things had really happened, or if they had both been dreaming the same bewildering dream.

Helena and Demetrius were by this time awake; and a sweet sleep having quieted Helena's disturbed and angry spirits, she listened with delight to the professions of love which Demetrius still made to her, and which, to her surprise as well as pleasure, she began to perceive were sincere.

These fair night-wandering ladies, now no longer rivals, became once more true friends; all the unkind words which had passed were forgiven, and they calmly consulted together what was best to be done in their present situation. It was soon agreed that, as Demetrius had given up his pretensions to Hermia, he should endeavor to prevail upon her father to revoke the cruel sentence of death that had been passed against her. Demetrius was preparing to return to Athens for this purpose, when they were surprised with the sight of Egeus, Hermia's father, who came to the wood in pursuit of his runaway daughter.

When Egeus understood that Demetrius would not now marry his daughter, he no longer opposed her marriage with Lysander, but gave his consent that they should be wedded on the fourth day from that time, being the same day on which Hermia had been condemned to lose her life; and on that same day Helena joyfully agreed to marry her beloved and now faithful Demetrius.

The fairy king and queen, who were invisible spectators of this reunion, and now saw the happy ending of the lovers' history, brought about through the good offices of Oberon, received so much pleasure that these kind spirits resolved to celebrate the approaching nuptials with sports and revels throughout their fairy kingdom.

And now, if any are offended with this story of fairies and their pranks, as judging it incredible and strange, they have only to think that they have been asleep and dreaming, and that all these adventures were visions which they saw in their sleep–and I hope none of my readers will be so unreasonable as to be offended with a pretty harmless Midsummer Night's Dream.

Puck's Song

William Shakespeare

Now the hungry lion roars,
And the wolf behowls the moon;
Whilst the heavy ploughman snores,
All with weary task fordone.
Now the wasted brands do glow,
Whilst the scritch-owl, scritching loud,
Puts the wretch that lies in woe
In remembrance of a shroud.
Now it is the time of night,
That the graves, all gaping wide,
Everyone lets forth his sprite,
In the church-way paths to glide:
And we fairies, that do run
By the triple Hecate's team,
From the presence of the sun,
Following darkness like a dream,
Now are frolic; not a mouse
Shall disturb this hallow'd house:
I am sent with broom before
To sweep the dust behind the door.

THE GRAY CUB

FROM *WHITE FANG*

JACK LONDON

He was different from his brothers and sisters. Their hair already betrayed the reddish hue inherited from their mother, the she-wolf; while he alone, in this particular, took after his father. He was the one little gray cub of the litter. He had bred true to the straight wolf-stock–in fact, he had bred true to old One Eye himself, physically, with but a single exception, and that was he had two eyes to his father's one.

The gray cub's eyes had not been open long, yet already he could see with steady clearness. And while his eyes were still closed, he had felt, tasted, and smelled. He knew his two brothers and his two sisters very well. He had begun to romp with them in a feeble, awkward way, and even to squabble, his little throat vibrating with a queer rasping noise (the forerunner of the growl), as he worked himself into a passion. And long before his eyes had opened he had learned by touch, taste, and smell to know his mother–a fount of warmth and liquid food and tenderness. She possessed a gentle, caressing tongue that soothed him when it passed over his soft little body, and that impelled him to snuggle close against her and to doze off to sleep.

Most of the first month of his life had been passed thus in sleeping; but now he could see quite well, and he stayed awake for longer periods of time, and he was coming to learn his world quite well. His world was gloomy; but he did not know that, for he knew no other world. It was dim-lighted; but his eyes had never had to adjust themselves to any other light. His world was very small. Its limits were the walls of the lair; but as he had no knowledge of the wide world outside, he was never oppressed by the narrow confines of his existence.

But he had early discovered that one wall of his world was different from the rest. This was the mouth of the cave and the source of light. He had discovered that it was different from the other walls long before he had any thoughts of his own, any conscious volitions. It had been an irresistible attraction before ever his eyes opened and looked upon it. The light from it had beat upon his sealed lids, and the eyes and the optic nerves had pulsated to little, spark-like flashes, warm-colored and strangely pleasing. The life of his body, and of every fiber of his body, the life that was the very substance of his body and that was apart from his own personal life, had yearned toward this light and urged his body toward it in the same way that the cunning chemistry of a plant urges it toward the sun.

Always, in the beginning, before his conscious life dawned, he had crawled toward the mouth of the cave. And in this his brothers and sisters were one with him. Never, in that period, did any of them crawl toward the dark corners of the back-wall. The light drew them as if they were plants; the chemistry of the life that composed them demanded the light as a necessity of being; and their little puppet-bodies crawled blindly and chemically, like the tendrils of a vine. Later on, when each developed individuality and became personally conscious of impulsions and desires, the attraction of the light increased. They were always crawling and sprawling toward it, and being driven back from it by their mother.

It was in this way that the gray cub learned other attributes of his mother than the soft, soothing, tongue. In his insistent crawling toward the light, he discovered in her a nose that with a sharp nudge administered rebuke, and later, a paw, that crushed him down and rolled him over and over with swift, calculating stroke. Thus he learned hurt; and on top of it he learned to avoid hurt, first, by not incurring the risk of it; and second, when he had incurred the risk, by dodging and by retreating. These were conscious actions, and were the results of his first generalizations upon the world. Before that he had recoiled automatically from hurt, as he had crawled automatically toward the light. After that he recoiled from hurt because he knew that it was hurt.

He was a fierce little cub. So were his brothers and sisters. It was to be expected. He was a carnivorous animal. He came of a breed of meat-killers and meat-eaters. His father and mother lived wholly upon meat. The milk he had sucked with his first flickering life, was milk transformed directly from meat, and now, at a month old, when his eyes had been open for but a week, he was beginning himself to eat meat—meat half-digested by the she-wolf and disgorged for the five growing cubs that already made too great demand upon her breast.

But he was, further, the fiercest of the litter. He could make a louder rasping growl than any of them. His tiny rages were much more terrible than theirs. It was he that first learned the trick of rolling a fellow cub over with a cunning paw-stroke. And it was he that first gripped another cub by the ear and pulled and tugged and growled through jaws tight-clenched. And certainly it was he that caused the mother the most trouble in keeping her litter from the mouth of the cave.

The fascination of the light for the gray cub increased from day to day. He was perpetually departing on yard-long adventures toward the cave's entrance, and as perpetually being driven back. Only he did not know it for an entrance. He did not know anything about entrances—passages whereby one goes from one place to another place. He did not know any other place, much less of a way to get there. So to him the entrance of the cave was a wall—a wall of light. As the sun was to the outside dweller, this wall was to him the sun of his world. It attracted him as a candle attracts a moth. He was always striving to attain it. The life that was so swiftly expanding within him urged him continually toward the wall of light. The life that was within him knew that it was the one way out, the way he was predestined to tread. But he himself did not know anything about it. He did not know there was any outside at all.

There was one strange thing about this wall of light. His father (he had already come to recognize his father as the one other dweller in the world, a creature like his mother, who slept near the light and was a bringer of meat)—his father had a way of walking right into the white far wall and disappearing. The gray cub could not understand this. Though never permitted by his mother to approach that wall, he had approached the other walls, and encountered hard obstruction on the end of his tender nose. This hurt. And after several such adventures, he left the walls alone. Without thinking about it, he accepted this disappearing into the wall as a peculiarity of his father, as milk and half-digested meat were peculiarities of his mother.

In fact, the gray cub was not given to thinking—at least, to the kind of thinking customary of men. His brain worked in dim ways. Yet his conclusions were as sharp and distinct as those achieved by men. He had a method of accepting things, without questioning the why and wherefore. In reality, this was the act of classification. He was never disturbed over why a thing happened. How it happened was sufficient for him. Thus, when he had bumped his nose on the back-wall a few times, he accepted that he would not disappear into walls. In the same way he accepted that his father could disappear into walls. But he was not in the least disturbed by desire to find out the reason for the difference between his father and himself. Logic and physics were no part of his mental make-up.

Like most creatures of the Wild, he early experienced famine. There came a time when not only did the meat-supply cease, but the milk no longer came from his mother's breast. At first, the cubs whimpered and cried, but for the most part they slept. It was not long before they were reduced to a coma of hunger. There were no more spats and squabbles, no more tiny rages nor attempts at growling; while the adventures toward the far white wall ceased altogether. The cubs slept, while the life that was in them flickered and died down.

One Eye was desperate. He ranged far and wide, and slept but little in the lair that had now become cheerless and miserable. The she-wolf, too, left her litter and went out in search of meat. In the first days after the birth of the cubs, One Eye had journeyed several times back to the Indian camp and robbed the rabbit snares; but, with the melting of the snow and the opening of the streams, the Indian camp had moved away, and that source of supply was closed to him.

When the gray cub came back to life and again took interest in the far white wall, he found that the population of his world had been reduced. Only one sister remained to him. The rest were gone. As he grew stronger, he found himself compelled to play alone, for the sister no longer lifted her head nor moved about. His little body rounded out with the meat he now ate; but the food had come too late for her. She slept continuously, a tiny skeleton flung round with skin in which the flame flickered lower and lower and at last went out.

Then there came a time when the gray cub no longer saw his father appearing and disappearing in the wall nor lying down asleep in the entrance. This had happened at the end of a second and less severe famine. The she-wolf knew why One Eye never came back, but there was no way by which she could tell what she had seen to the gray cub. Hunting herself for meat, up the left fork of the stream where lived the lynx, she had followed a day-old trail of One Eye. And she had found him, or what remained of him, at the end of the trail. There were many signs of the battle that had been fought, and of the lynx's withdrawal to her lair after having won the victory.

Before she went away, the she-wolf had found this lair, but the signs told her that the lynx was inside, and she had not dared to venture in.

After that, the she-wolf in her hunting avoided the left fork. For she knew that in the lynx's lair was a litter of kittens, and she knew the lynx for a fierce, bad-tempered creature and a terrible fighter. It was all very well for half a dozen wolves to drive a lynx, spitting and bristling, up a tree; but it was quite a different matter for a lone wolf to encounter a lynx–especially when the lynx was known to have a litter of hungry kittens at her back.

But the Wild is the Wild, and motherhood is motherhood, at all times fiercely protective whether in the Wild or out of it; and the time was to come when the she-wolf, for her gray cub's sake, would venture the left fork, and the lair in the rocks, and the lynx's wrath.

The Frogs Who Wished for A King

Aesop

The Frogs were living as happy as could be in a marshy swamp that just suited them; they went splashing about caring for nobody and nobody troubling with them. But some of them thought that this was not right, that they should have a king and a proper constitution, so they determined to send up a petition to Jove to give them what they wanted.

"Mighty Jove," they cried, "send us a king that will rule over us and keep us in order." Jove laughed at their croaking, and threw down into the swamp a huge Log, which came down–*kersplash!*

The Frogs were frightened out of their skins by the commotion made in their midst, and all rushed to the bank to look at the horrible monster. But after a time, seeing that it did not move, one or two of the boldest of them ventured out towards the Log, and even dared to touch it. Still it did not move. Then the greatest hero of the Frogs jumped upon the Log and began dancing up and down upon it. Soon all the Frogs came and did the same; and for some time the Frogs went about their business every day without taking the slightest notice of their new King Log lying in their midst.

But this did not suit them, so they sent another petition to Jove, and said to him, "We want a real king; one that will really rule over us." Now this made Jove angry, so he sent among them a big Stork that soon set to work gobbling them all up. Then the Frogs repented–but too late.

"Better no rule than cruel rule."

A Good Play

Robert Louis Stevenson

We built a ship upon the stairs
All made of the back-bedroom chairs,
And filled it full of sofa pillows
To go a-sailing on the billows.

We took a saw and several nails,
And water in the nursery pails,
And Tom said, "Let us also take
An apple and a slice of cake–"
Which was enough for Tom and me
To go a-sailing on, till tea.

We sailed along for days and days,
And had the very best of plays;
But Tom fell out and hurt his knee,
So there was no one left but me.

SHIPWRECKED!

FROM *THE SWISS FAMILY ROBINSON*

JOHANN DAVID WYSS

For six days the storm had raged wildly, and our situation became more dangerous every hour. Driven out of our course, we no longer knew our position, and the ship had lost her masts and was leaking.

Down in our cabin my four sons clung fearfully to their mother, and to all of us it seemed that the end was near. Then, suddenly, came a cry from above–"Land! Land!" But almost at the same moment we felt a sudden shock that seemed to shake the vessel asunder, followed by a fearful crash. With sinking heart I realized that we had struck a rock.

"Lower the boats!" I heard the captain shout.

Hurrying on deck, I was startled to see that the ship's boats were already dangerously overcrowded, and that it would be almost impossible for us to find places. Buffeted by the wind and half-blinded by the spray, I crossed to the side of the vessel, but I was only in time to see the last rope cut, and the next moment a mighty wave had separated the boats from us, and had driven them far beyond our reach. In my despair I shouted wildly for help, imploring them to return, but my voice was lost amid the roar of the storm, and soon nothing was to be seen of the retreating boats but two dark specks that now and again appeared on the white surface of the ocean.

All chance of escape now seemed gone for ever, and I was about to resign myself to certain death, when, turning my eyes southward, I was overjoyed to perceive a coastline stretching along the horizon. Thither, from that time, all my hopes were directed.

My family, who had heard my cries for help, rushed on deck, and their anguish, when they realized our situation, was greater than my own had been. Forgetting our real helplessness in my newborn hope of reaching the island which I had just discovered, I tried to reassure them.

"Take courage!" I said. "Our cabin is so fixed as to be beyond the reach of the waves, and land is not far off. If the storm should abate during the night, it is possible that we might reach it."

My children, with the confidence of their age, now cast their fears aside, and looked forward joyfully to certain deliverance on the morrow. As the evening advanced the storm increased in violence. My three youngest children, who were quite exhausted by the anxieties of the day, fell fast asleep; but Ernest, my eldest boy, who was able fully to comprehend the dangers of our position, remained up with me to help me in my search after bladders, casks, or anything that would serve as buoys, by means of which we might reach the land should the vessel break up during the night.

Having found several empty kegs, and having joined them firmly together in pairs, we fastened them under our arms and thus we hoped, in case of emergency, to float ashore. These precautions taken, Ernest too was overcome by fatigue, and my wife and I were left alone to pass the night in prayer.

As morning dawned the storm began to abate; the sea became calmer; the wind fell, and a glorious sun shed his golden rays over the troubled surface of the waters. Delighted by the change, I summoned the boys on deck.

Ernest, who was always ready for instant action, proposed that we should explore the ship, as we were sure to find many things on board which would be of use to us should we ever reach land. Acting on his suggestion, I sent them all on a voyage of discovery to the hold of the vessel, and as they started eagerly on their mission each vowed to bring back just the thing that was most required.

A few minutes after I heard a cry of "Papa, they'll bite me! I'm afraid!" and saw little Jack appearing on deck holding on bravely to the collars of two huge dogs, which were making frantic efforts to jump on him and lick his face. This was their manner of testifying their gratitude to their deliverer, who had found the poor half-famished brutes shut up in the captain's cabin.

"Well, Jack," I said, as I relieved him of his charge; "I don't think your discovery will benefit us much at any rate."

"I know that, papa," he answered, ruefully; "but the poor animals looked so hungry, I could not find it in my heart to leave them below; besides, they will be very useful to us for hunting when we get on land."

"You are right," I said, "but have you thought of how we are to get there?"

"Oh yes!" he replied. "I have heard of people making rafts at sea, and have been thinking that we might do the same if we could find some boards and ropes."

"A very good idea, Jack, and one we must try to carry out; but here come the others! Let us see how their search has been rewarded."

When the boys displayed their treasures, I was quite astonished to see the number of useful things which they had collected, and how wisely their selection had been made with a view to our future wants. Amongst other things I noticed, with joy, fowling-pieces, fish-hooks, powder and balls–for I knew that on these we should be dependent for our food; nails, hammers, saws, gimlets, and other carpenters' tools had likewise not been forgotten. As for my wife, she announced triumphantly that she had found a cow, some sheep, and several goats just in time to save their lives, for, as they had been neglected during the storm, they were almost famished.

We now began to think of constructing a raft, by means of which we might reach the island, which, since the clouds had partially cleared away, could be distinctly seen against the horizon; and we all started for the hold again in search of anything that could make do in service as a boat.

The only things to be found, which were at all suitable for our purpose, were four wooden casks firmly bound with iron. These we sawed in halves, and having placed the eight tubs side by side and joined them tightly together, we nailed them to a strong plank. Two other planks were then fastened along the sides of the tubs and brought to a point at each end, so that the raft might cut the water easily; while, to prevent its being overturned, a balancing pole, to which some empty brandy casks were tied, was fixed at each end of the strange vessel, and the work was completed.

With some difficulty, and not without help from a powerful lever I found on board, we launched our bark. The children, who felt very proud of their handiwork, were anxious to embark immediately, but, as the evening was advanced, I decided to remain on the wreck another night, and try to reach land on the following day, should it be sufficiently calm.

The sun shone brightly the next morning, and everything seemed to favor our removal, so, gathering together whatever we thought might be useful to us in the future, we were about to trust our lives to the raft, when the crowing of the cocks, which we were leaving behind, attracted our attention. At their mother's request the children returned for the hens and pigeons, which they placed in a large wicker cage, while the ducks and geese were set at liberty in the hope that instinct would guide them to land. Having carefully provided the animals on board with food and drink enough to last them several days, and having loaded the boat with ammunition, food, carpenters' tools, canvas for making our tent, and as many other useful things as I could make room for, we embarked. My wife occupied the first tub; in the second sat Jack, a boy of eight years of age; in the third the six-year-old Franz; the powder, sailcloth, and fowls were stowed away in the fourth; the victuals in the fifth; the sixth held Fritz, now fourteen years old; the seventh, Ernest, who had just attained his sixteenth year; while I occupied the eighth, and endeavored by means of a pole to steer our wonderful vessel.

As the dogs, Topsy and Bill, which had been left on the wreck, saw the raft slowly retreating, they sprang whining into the water and soon overtook us. But as, on account of their size, it would have been dangerous to take them on board, they swam after us, now and again resting themselves by placing their forepaws on the casks that were fastened to the balancing poles. Thus we reached the island.

From a distance it presented a very barren appearance, and nothing could be seen but a line of rocks extending the whole length of the coast. On a nearer approach, however, trees, which we guessed to be palms, were visible not far from the water's edge; and by the aid of a small telescope, which Jack produced from his pocket with no small amount of pride, I could see that the land was not nearly so sterile and uninviting as we had at first feared. A little creek which served as a landing-place was soon discovered, and at last we set foot on the welcome soil.

Our next anxiety was to find a suitable place to erect a tent where we might pass the night in safety. Not long after this also was found, and soon, by means of poles, which we fastened in the fissures of the rocks, and sail-cloth, with which we had provided ourselves before leaving the wreck, our temporary habitation was constructed. Some moss and withered grass, which the boys had gathered and spread out in the sun to dry, furnished us with pillows, and our arrangements for passing the night were complete.

While the boys were occupying themselves inside the tent, I collected a pile of stones on the margin of a stream that ran near us, and built a sort of fireplace, in which a huge fire of dried sticks and twigs was soon crackling pleasantly. My wife, with the goal of appeasing our hunger, placed on the rude grate a pot of water, into which I threw a few pieces of the portable soup that we had found among the cook's possessions; and soon the savory odor of the preparation told us we might expect a palatable dinner, for which we were beginning to feel the necessity.

Meanwhile Fritz, who had been well accustomed to the use of firearms among our native mountains in Switzerland, loaded his gun and proceeded along the banks of the stream which flowed close by, in search of something with which to stock our larder; Ernest also set out, but preferred to take the opposite direction; while Jack, who was less ambitious than the others, contented himself with climbing the rocks in search of mussels, for which he had a strong preference.

They had not been long gone when I heard a cry of terror, and, seizing my axe, I rushed in the direction of the sound, expecting to find that Jack had got into some new mischief. The sight that met my eyes, however was more laughable than terrifying, but my appearance was evidently a relief to the boy, who called out when he saw me approaching, "Papa, papa! Please come fast; I have caught a terrible animal." Looking into the water, in which he stood up to his knees, it struck me that the "terrible animal" had caught him rather than he it, for a huge lobster held him tightly by the leg, and all his efforts to free himself from its clutches were fruitless.

A slight blow from my hatchet soon made it release its hold, however, and catching it by the back I brought it on shore, much to the delight of the other boys, whom their brother's cry of terror had summoned to the rescue.

Now that all danger of another attack from the enemy seemed over, Jack, burning with anxiety to be the bearer of the prisoner to his mother, caught it eagerly with both hands; but scarcely had he touched it, when he received a sharp blow on the face from its tail. A renewed howl of anger and fright burst from him as he threw the lobster violently on the ground, and vowed never again to touch the "ugly brute." Taking the animal again by the middle of the body, I showed him how his own carelessness had brought its punishment, and that by holding it properly it could be rendered quite harmless.

Having shown my wife what Jack proudly called his "captive," Ernest suggested that it should be utilized at once and thrown into the pot, as it would much improve the flavor of the soup. Our housekeeper, however, did not look favorably on the recipe, and preferred to reserve the animal for future use. She suggested to Ernest, though, that if he wished to make our meal more enjoyable, he should procure a little salt, as that was the only ingredient the soup now required in order to make it palatable. He ran off quickly in search of this valuable commodity, which he assured us he could easily find, as he had seen it lying in handfuls in the fissures of the rocks where the sun had dried the seawater.

He proved his assertion, too, by bringing back a good quantity of the desired seasoning, but it was so mixed with sand and seaweed that I immediately pronounced it useless. My wife, however, dissolved it in fresh water, and, having filtered it through a piece of canvas, managed to improve the flavor of our dinner wonderfully.

At last our meal was ready, and we gathered eagerly round the pot, anxious to satisfy our appetites, which the morning's work had made ravenous. But a new difficulty then presented itself. The soup was ready to be eaten, and we were anxious to eat it, but without plates and spoons, or anything to function in their places, how were we to manage?

"If we had some coconuts," suggested Ernest, "we could make spoons from their shells."

"Quite true," I answered, gravely; "and if we had a china dinner set and a dozen soup ladles we might handle our difficulty beautifully, but the one is as much beyond our reach as the other."

"How would mussel shells serve our purpose?' asked my wife. "I saw Jack playing with some a little while ago–perhaps they might do."

"Capitally," I replied, "if we can only get some. Jack might lead the way to where they may be found."

The children ran off and soon returned bringing a good supply, and this difficulty now overcome, we sat down thankfully to our first meal in our new home.

Soon the sun sank behind the horizon, and the darkness that immediately followed showed me that we must be near the equator. The increasing chilliness of the air warned us to take shelter in the tent, whose protection from the cutting night wind that had suddenly sprung up was exceedingly welcome. The storm had now completely abated, and the sea, as if exhausted by its own fury, lay calm as a lake.

Poor Old Lady

Traditional

Poor old lady, she swallowed a fly.
I don't know why she swallowed a fly.
Poor old lady, I think she'll die.

Poor old lady, she swallowed a spider.
It squirmed and wriggled and turned inside her.
She swallowed the spider to catch the fly.
I don't know why she swallowed a fly.
Poor old lady, I think she'll die.

Poor old lady, she swallowed a bird.
How absurd! She swallowed a bird.
She swallowed the bird to catch the spider,
She swallowed the spider to catch the fly,
I don't know why she swallowed a fly.
Poor old lady, I think she'll die.

Poor old lady, she swallowed a cat.
Think of that! She swallowed a cat.
She swallowed the cat to catch the bird.
She swallowed the bird to catch the spider,
She swallowed the spider to catch the fly,
I don't know why she swallowed a fly.
Poor old lady, I think she'll die.

Poor old lady, she swallowed a dog.
She went the whole hog when she swallowed the dog.
She swallowed the dog to catch the cat,
She swallowed the cat to catch the bird,
She swallowed the bird to catch the spider.
She swallowed the spider to catch the fly,
I don't know why she swallowed a fly.
Poor old lady, I think she'll die.

Poor old lady, she swallowed a cow.
I don't know how she swallowed the cow.
She swallowed the cow to catch the dog,
She swallowed the dog to catch the cat,
She swallowed the cat to catch the bird,
She swallowed the bird to catch the spider,
She swallowed the spider to catch the fly,
I don't know why she swallowed a fly.
Poor old lady, I think she'll die.

Poor old lady, she swallowed a horse.
She died, of course.

The Duel

Eugene Field

The gingham dog and the calico cat
Side by side on the table sat;
'Twas half-past twelve, and (what do you think!)
Nor one nor t'other had slept a wink!
    The old Dutch clock and the Chinese plate
    Appeared to know so sure as fate
There was going to be a terrible spat.
    (I wasn't there; I simply state
    What was told to me by the Chinese plate!)

The gingham dog went "bow-wow-wow!"
And the calico cat replied "mee-ow!"
The air was littered, an hour or so,
With bits of gingham and calico,
    While the old Dutch clock in the chimney-place
    Up with its hands before its face,

For it always dreaded a family row!
(Now mind: I'm only telling you
What the old Dutch clock declares is true!)

The Chinese plate looked very blue,
And wailed, "Oh, dear! what shall we do!"
But the gingham dog and the calico cat
Wallowed this way and tumbled that,
Employing every tooth and claw
In the awfullest way you ever saw–
And, oh! how the gingham and calico flew!
(Don't fancy I exaggerate–
I got my news from the Chinese plate!)

Next morning, where the two had sat
They found no trace of dog or cat;
And some folks think unto this day
That burglars stole that pair away!
But the truth about the cat and pup
Is this: they ate each other up!
Now what do you really think of that!
(The old Dutch clock it told me so,
And that is how I came to know.)

Down the Rabbit-Hole

From *Alice's Adventures in Wonderland*

Lewis Carroll

Alice was beginning to get very tired of sitting by her sister on the bank, and of having nothing to do: once or twice she had peeped into the book her sister was reading, but it had no pictures or conversations in it, "and what is the use of a book," thought Alice, "without pictures or conversations?"

So she was considering in her own mind (as well as she could, for the hot day made her feel very sleepy and stupid,) whether the pleasure of making a daisy-chain would be worth the trouble of getting up and picking the daisies, when suddenly a white rabbit with pink eyes ran close by her.

There was nothing so *very* remarkable in that; nor did Alice think it so *very* much out of the way to hear the Rabbit say to itself, "Oh dear! Oh dear! I shall be too late" (when she thought it over afterwards, it occurred to her that she ought to have wondered at this, but at the time it all seemed quite natural); but when the Rabbit actually *took a watch out of its waistcoat-pocket,* and looked at it, and then hurried on, Alice started to her feet, for it flashed across her mind that she had never before seen a rabbit with either a waistcoat-pocket or a watch to take out of it, and, burning with curiosity, she ran across the field after it, and was just in time to see it pop down a large rabbit-hole under the hedge.

In another moment down went Alice after it, never once considering how in the world she was to get out again.

The rabbit-hole went straight on like a tunnel for some way, and then dipped suddenly down, so suddenly that Alice had not a moment to think about stopping herself before she found herself falling down what seemed to be a very deep well.

Either the well was very deep, or she fell very slowly, for she had plenty of time as she went down to look about her, and to wonder what was going to happen next. First, she tried to look down and make out what she was coming to, but it was too dark to see anything: then she looked at the sides of the well, and noticed that they were filled with cupboards and book-shelves–here and there she saw maps and pictures hung upon pegs. She took down a jar from one of the shelves as she passed; it was labeled, "ORANGE MARMALADE," but to her great disappointment it was empty. She did not like to drop the jar for fear of killing somebody underneath, so managed to put it into one of the cupboards as she fell past it.

"Well!" thought Alice to herself, "after such a fall as this, I shall think nothing of tumbling down stairs! How brave they'll all think me at home! Why, I wouldn't say anything about it, even if I fell off the top of the house" (Which was very likely true.)

Down, down, down. Would the fall *never* come to an end? "I wonder how many miles I've fallen by this time?" she said aloud. "I must be getting somewhere near the center of the earth. Let me see–that would be four thousand miles down, I think–" (for, you see, Alice had learnt several things of this sort in her lessons in the schoolroom, and though this was not a *very* good opportunity for showing off her knowledge, as there was no one to listen to her, still it was good practice to say it over) "–yes, that's about the right distance–but then I wonder what Latitude or Longitude I've got to?"

(Alice had not the slightest idea what Latitude was, or Longitude either, but she thought they were nice grand words to say.)

Presently she began again. "I wonder if I shall fall right *through* the earth! How funny it'll seem to come out among the people that walk with their heads downwards! The Antipathies, I think–" (she was rather glad there was no one listening, this time, as it didn't sound at all the right word) "–but I shall have to ask them what the name of the country is, you know. Please, Ma'am, is this New Zealand or Australia?" (and she tried to curtsey as she spoke–fancy *curtseying* as you're falling through the air! Do you think you could manage it?) "And what an ignorant little girl she'll think me for asking! No, it'll never do to ask–perhaps I shall see it written up somewhere."

Down, down, down. There was nothing else to do, so Alice soon began talking again. "Dinah'll miss me very much to-night, I should think!" (Dinah was the cat.) "I hope they'll remember her saucer of milk at tea-time. Dinah, my dear! I wish you were down here with me! There are no mice in the air, I'm afraid, but you might catch a bat, and that's very like a mouse, you know. But do cats eat bats, I wonder?" And here Alice began to get rather sleepy, and went on saying to herself, in a dreamy sort of way, "Do cats eat bats? Do cats eat bats?" and sometimes, "Do bats eat cats?" for, you see, as she couldn't answer either question, it didn't much matter which way she put it. She felt that she was dozing off, and had just begun to dream that she was walking hand in hand with Dinah, and was saying to her very earnestly, "Now, Dinah, tell me the truth: did you ever eat a bat?" when suddenly, thump! thump! down she came upon a heap of sticks and dry leaves, and the fall was over.

Alice was not a bit hurt, and she jumped up on to her feet in a moment: she looked up, but it was all dark overhead; before her was another long passage, and the White Rabbit was still in sight, hurrying down it. There was not a moment to be lost–away went Alice like the wind, and was just in time to hear it say, as it turned a corner, "Oh my ears and whiskers, how late it's getting!" She was close behind it when she turned the corner, but the Rabbit was no longer to be seen: she found herself in a long, low hall, which was lit up by a row of lamps hanging from the roof.

There were doors all around the hall, but they were all locked, and when Alice had been all the way down one side and up the other, trying every door, she walked sadly down the middle, wondering how she was ever to get out again.

Suddenly she came upon a little three-legged table, all made of solid glass; there was nothing on it but a tiny golden key, and Alice's first idea was that this might belong to one of the doors of the hall; but alas! either the locks were too large, or the key was too small, but at any rate it would not open any of them. However, on the second time round, she came upon a low curtain she had not noticed before, and behind it was a little door about fifteen inches high; she tried the little golden key in the lock, and to her great delight it fitted!

Alice opened the door and found that it led into a small passage, not much larger than a rathole. She knelt down and looked along the passage into the loveliest garden you ever saw. How she longed to get out of the dark hall, and wander about among those beds of bright flowers and those cool fountains, but she could not even get her head through the doorway; "and even if my head *would* go through," thought poor Alice, "it would be of very little use without my shoulders. Oh, how I wish I could shut up like a telescope! I think I could, if I only knew how to begin." For, you see, so many out-of-the-way things had happened lately that Alice had begun to think that very few things indeed were really impossible.

There seemed to be no use in waiting by the little door, so she went back to the table, half hoping she might find another key on it, or at any rate a book of rules for shutting people up like telescopes. This time she found a little bottle on it, ("which certainly was not here before," said Alice,) and tied round the neck of the bottle was a paper label with the words "DRINK ME" beautifully printed on it in large letters.

It was all very well to say "Drink me," but the wise little Alice was not going to do *that* in a hurry. "No, I'll look first," she said, "and see whether it's marked '*poison*' or not," for she had read several nice little stories about children who had got burnt, and eaten up by wild beasts, and other unpleasant things, all because they would not remember the simple rules their friends had taught them, such as, that a red-hot poker will burn you if you hold it too long; and that if you cut your finger *very* deeply with a knife, it usually bleeds; and she had never forgotten that, if you drink much from a bottle marked "poison," it is almost certain to disagree with you, sooner or later.

However, this bottle was *not* marked "poison," so Alice ventured to taste it, and finding it very nice, (it had, in fact, a sort of mixed flavor of cherry-tart, custard, pineapple, roast turkey, toffee, and hot buttered toast,) she very soon finished it off.

"What a curious feeling!" said Alice, "I must be shutting up like a telescope."

And so it was indeed: she was now only ten inches high, and her face brightened up at the thought that she was now the right size for going through the little door into that lovely garden. First, however, she waited for a few minutes to see if she was going to shrink any further. She felt a little nervous about this, "for it might end, you know," said Alice to herself, "in my going out altogether, like a candle. I wonder what I should be like then?" And she tried to fancy what the flame of a candle looks like after the candle is blown out, for she could not remember ever having seen such a thing.

After a while, finding that nothing more happened, she decided on going into the garden at once, but, alas for poor Alice! When she got to the door, she found she had forgotten the little golden key, and when she went back to the table for it, she found she could not possibly reach it: she could see it quite plainly through the glass, and she tried her best to climb up one of the legs of the table, but it was too slippery, and when she had tired herself out with trying, the poor little thing sat down and cried.

"Come, there's no use in crying like that!" said Alice to herself, rather sharply, "I advise you to leave off this minute!" She generally gave herself very good advice, (though she very seldom followed it,) and sometimes she scolded herself so severely as to bring tears into her eyes, and once she remembered trying to box her own ears for having cheated herself in a game of croquet she was playing against herself, for this curious child was very fond of pretending to be two people. "But it's no use now," thought poor Alice, "to pretend to be two people! Why, there's hardly enough of me left to make *one* respectable person!"

Soon her eye fell on a little glass box that was lying under the table: she opened it, and found in it a very small cake, on which the words "EAT ME" were beautifully marked in currants.

"Well, I'll eat it," said Alice, "and if it makes me grow larger, I can reach the key; and if it makes me grow smaller, I can creep under the door; so either way I'll get into the garden, and I don't care which happens!"

She ate a little bit, and said anxiously to herself "Which way? Which way?" holding her hand on the top of her head to feel which way it was growing, and she was quite surprised to find that she remained the same size. To be sure, this is what generally happens when one eats cake, but Alice had got so much into the way of expecting nothing but out-of-the-way things to happen, that it seemed quite dull and stupid for life to go on in the common way.

So she set to work, and very soon finished off the cake.

BELLING THE CAT

AESOP

Long ago, the mice had a general council to consider what measures they could take to outwit their common enemy, the Cat. Some said this, and some said that; but at last a young mouse got up and said he had a proposal to make, which he thought would solve the problem.

"You will all agree," said he, "that our chief danger consists in the sly and treacherous manner in which the enemy approaches us. Now, if we could receive some signal of her approach, we could easily escape from her. I venture, therefore, to propose that a small bell be found, and attached by a ribbon round the neck of the Cat. By this means we should always know when she was about, and could easily retire while she was in the neighborhood."

This proposal met with general applause, until an old mouse got up and said: "That is all very well, but who is to bell the Cat?" The mice looked at one another and nobody spoke. Then the old mouse said:

"It is easy to propose impossible remedies."

Riddle Me This . . .

1. How many letters are in "the alphabet"?

2. I soar without wings,
   I see without eyes.
   I've traveled the universe to and fro.
   I've conquered the world,
   Yet I've never been anywhere but home.
   Who am I?

3. What do the following three have in common?
   Superman
   Moses
   The Cabbage Patch Kids

4. What is black when it's new,
   Red when you use it,
   And gray when you throw it away?

5. Name three consecutive days without using the words Monday, Tuesday, Wednesday, Thursday, Friday, Saturday, or Sunday.

6. I can sizzle like bacon,
   I am made with an egg,
   I have plenty of backbone, but lack a good leg,
   I peel layers like onions, but still remain whole,
   I can be long, like a flagpole, yet fit in a hole.
   What am I?

7. I am the only thing that always tells the truth.
   I show off everything that I see.
   I come in all shapes and sizes.
   So tell me what I must be!

8. Pronounced as one letter,
   But look and you'll see,
   That really I'm written with three.
   When read from both ends,
   I'm the same either way.
   What am I?

9. The higher I climb,
   The hotter I become,
   But I cannot escape my crystal cage.
   What am I?

10. First I'm green,
    Later I'm brown,
    Both of these times make people frown.
    But just in between,
    For a very short while,
    I'm perfect and yellow,
    And make people smile!
    What am I?

11. When I point up everything is bright,
    But when I point down all becomes dark.
    What am I?

12. Many things can make me.
    I can be of any shape or size.
    I am created for many reasons,
    And I can shrink or grow with time.
    What am I?

13. I always point in the right direction.
    Disobey me and pay the consequences.
    My instructions are as clear as black and white,
    But I never say more than two words at a time.
    What am I?

14. What kind of coat can be put on only when wet?

15. What didn't Adam and Eve have that everyone else has?

16. I'm not an airplane,
But I can fly through the sky.
I'm not a river,
But I'm full of water.
What am I?

17. I am as cold as death,
But always breathing.
Never thirsty,
But always drinking.
Covered in mail,
But never clinking.
What am I?

18. I am used to bat with,
Yet I never get a hit.
I am near a ball,
But it is never thrown.
What am I?

19. From house to house I go,
    A messenger small and slight.
    And whether it rains or snows,
    I always sleep outside at night.
    What am I?

20. Dark with white markings,
    And smooth like a rock.
    Where learning occurs,
    I help convey thought.
    What am I?

21. I can be cracked,
    I can be made.
    I can be told,
    I can be played.
    What am I?

Answers:

1) There are 11 letters in "The Alphabet." Did you say 26? 2) Your imagination. 3) They were all adopted. 4) Charcoal. 5) Yesterday, Today, and Tomorrow. 6) A snake. 7) A Mirror. 8) The word "eye." 9) Mercury in a thermometer. 10) A Banana. 11) A Light Switch. 12) A Hole. 13) A "One Way" sign. 14) A coat of paint. 15) Parents. 16) A Cloud. 17) A Fish. 18) Your Eyelashes! 19) A Road. 20) A Blackboard. 21) A Joke!

How the Animals Lost Their Tails and Got Them Back Traveling From Philadelphia to Medicine Hat

Carl Sandburg

Far up in North America, near the Saskatchewan river, in the Winnipeg wheat country, not so far from the town of Moose Jaw named for the jaw of a moose shot by a hunter there, up where the blizzards and the chinooks begin, where nobody works unless they have to and they nearly all have to, there stands the place known as Medicine Hat.

And there on a high stool in a high tower on a high hill sits the Head Spotter of the Weather Makers.

When the animals lost their tails it was because the Head Spotter of the Weather Makers at Medicine Hat was careless.

The tails of the animals were stiff and dry because for a long while there was dusty dry weather. Then at last came rain. And the water from the sky poured on the tails of the animals and softened them.

Then the chilly chills came whistling with icy mittens and they froze all the tails stiff. A big wind blew up and blew and blew till all the tails of the animals blew off.

It was easy for the fat stub hogs with their fat stub tails. But it was not so easy for the blue fox who uses his tail to help him when he runs, when he eats, when he walks or talks, when he makes pictures or writes letters in the snow or when he puts a snack of bacon meat with stripes of fat and lean to hide till he wants it under a big rock by a river.

It was easy enough for the rabbit who has long ears and no tail at all except a white thumb of cotton. But it was hard for the yellow flongboo who at night lights up his house in a hollow tree with his fire yellow torch of a tail. It is hard for the yellow flongboo to lose his tail because it lights up his way when he sneaks at night on the prairie, sneaking up on the flangwayers, the hippers and hangjasts, so good to eat.

The animals picked a committee of representatives to represent them in a parleyhoo to see what steps could be taken by talking to do something. There were sixty-six representatives on the committee and they decided to call it the Committee of Sixty-Six. It was a distinguished committee and when they all sat together holding their mouths under their noses (just like a distinguished committee) and blinking their eyes up over their noses and cleaning their ears and scratching themselves under the chin looking thoughtful (just like a distinguished committee) then anybody would say just to look at them, "This must be quite a distinguished committee."

Of course, they would all have looked more distinguished if they had had their tails on. If the big wavy streak of a blue tail blows off behind a blue fox, he doesn't look nearly so distinguished. Or, if the long yellow torch of a tail blows off behind a yellow flongboo, he doesn't look so distinguished as he did before the wind blew.

So the Committee of Sixty-Six had a meeting and a parleyhoo to decide what steps could be taken by talking to do something. For chairman they picked an old flongboo who was an umpire and used to umpire many mix-ups. Among the flongboos he was called "the umpire of umpires," "the king of umpires," "the prince of umpires," "the peer of umpires." When there was a fight and a snag and a wrangle between two families living next-door neighbors to each other and this old flongboo was called in to umpire and to say which family was right and which family was wrong, which family started it and which family ought to stop it, he used to say, "The best umpire is the one who knows just how far to go and how far not to go." He was from Massachusetts, born near Chappaquiddick, this old flongboo, and he lived there in a horse chestnut tree six feet thick halfway between South Hadley and Northampton. And at night, before he lost his tail, he lighted up the big hollow cave inside the horse chestnut tree with his yellow torch of a tail.

After he was nominated with speeches and elected with votes to be the chairman, he stood up on the platform and took a gavel and banged with the gavel and made the Committee of Sixty-Six come to order.

"It is no picnic to lose your tail and we are here for business," he said, banging his gavel again.

A blue fox from Waco, Texas, with his ears full of dry bluebonnet leaves from a hole where he lived near the Brazos river, stood up and said, "Mr. Chairman, do I have the floor?"

"You have whatever you get away with–I get your number," said the chairman.

"I make a motion," said the blue fox from Waco, "and I move you, Sir, that this committee get on a train at Philadelphia and ride on the train till it stops and then take another train and take more trains and keep on riding till we get to Medicine Hat, near the Saskatchewan river, in the Winnipeg wheat country where the Head Spotter of the Weather Makers sits on a high stool in a high tower on a high hill spotting the weather. There we will ask him if he will respectfully let us beseech him to bring back weather that will bring back our tails. It was the weather took away our tails; it is the weather can bring back our tails."

"All in favor of the motion," said the chairman, "will clean their right ears with their right paws."

And all the blue foxes and all the yellow flongboos began cleaning their right ears with their right paws.

"All who are against the motion will clean their left ears with their left paws," said the chairman.

And all the blue foxes and all the yellow flongboos began cleaning their left ears with their left paws.

"The motion is carried both ways–it is a razmataz," said the chairman. "Once again, all in favor of the motion will stand up on the toes of their hind legs and stick their noses straight up in the air." And all the blue foxes and all the yellow flongboos stood up on the toes of their hind legs and stuck their noses straight up in the air.

"And now," said the chairman, "all who are against the motion will stand on the top and the apex of their heads, stick their hind legs straight up in the air, and make a noise like a woof woof."

And then not one of the blue foxes and not one of the yellow flongboos stood on the top and the apex of his head nor stuck his hind legs up in the air nor made a noise like a woof woof.

"The motion is carried and this is no picnic," said the chairman.

So the committee went to Philadelphia to get on a train to ride on.

"Would you be so kind as to tell us the way to the union depot," the chairman asked a policeman. It was the first time a flongboo ever spoke to a policeman on the streets of Philadelphia.

"It pays to be polite," said the policeman.

"May I ask you again if you would kindly direct us to the union depot? We wish to ride on a train," said the flongboo.

"Polite persons and angry persons are different kinds," said the policeman.

The flongboo's eyes changed their lights and a slow torch of fire sprang out behind where his tail used to be. And speaking to the policeman, he said, "Sir, I must inform you, publicly and respectfully, that we are The Committee of Sixty-Six. We are honorable and distinguished representatives from places your honest and ignorant geography never told you about. This committee is going to ride on the cars to Medicine Hat near the Saskatchewan river in the Winnipeg wheat country where the blizzards and chinooks begin. We have a special message and a secret errand for the Head Spotter of the Weather Makers."

"I am a polite friend of all respectable people–that is why I wear this star to arrest people who are not respectable," said the policeman, touching with his pointed finger the silver and nickel star fastened with a safety pin on his blue uniform coat.

"This is the first time ever in the history of the United States that a committee of sixty-six blue foxes and flongboos has ever visited a city in the United States," insinuated the flongboo.

"I beg to be mistaken," finished the policeman. "The union depot is under that clock." And he pointed to a clock nearby.

"I thank you for myself, I thank you for the Committee of Sixty-Six, I thank you for the sake of all the animals in the United States who have lost their tails," finished the chairman.

Over to the Philadelphia union depot they went, all sixty-six, half blue foxes, half flongboos. As they pattered pitty-pat, pitty-pat, each with feet and toenails, ears and hair, everything but tails, into the Philadelphia union depot, they had nothing to say. And yet though they had nothing to say, the passengers in the union depot waiting for trains thought they had something to say and were saying it. So the passengers in the union depot waiting for trains listened. But with all their listening the passengers never heard the blue foxes and yellow flongboos say anything.

"They are saying it to each other in some strange language from where they belong," said one passenger waiting for a train.

"They have secrets to keep among each other, and never tell us," said another passenger.

"We will find out all about it reading the newspapers upside down tomorrow morning," said a third passenger.

Then the blue foxes and the yellow flongboos pattered pitty-pat, pitty-pat, each with feet and toenails, ears and hair, everything except tails, pattered scritch scratch over the stone floors out into the train shed. They climbed into a special smoking car hooked on ahead of the engine.

"This car hooked on ahead of the engine was put on special for us so we will always be ahead and we will get there before the train does," said the chairman to the committee.

The train ran out of the train shed. It kept on the tracks and never left the rails. It came to the Horseshoe Curve near Altoona where the tracks bend like a big horseshoe. Instead of going around the long winding bend of the horseshoe tracks up and around the mountains, the train acted different. The train jumped off the tracks down into the valley and cut across in a straight line on a cut-off, jumped on the tracks again and went on toward Ohio.

The conductor said, "If you are going to jump the train off the tracks, tell us about it beforehand."

"When we lost our tails nobody told us about it beforehand," said the old flongboo umpire.

Two baby blue foxes, the youngest on the committee, sat on the front platform. Mile after mile of chimneys went by. Four hundred smokestacks stood in a row and tubs on tubs of sooty black soot marched out.

"This is the place where the black cats come to be washed," said the first baby blue fox.

"I believe your affidavit," said the second blue fox.

Crossing Ohio and Indiana at night the flongboos took off the roof of the car. The conductor told them, "I must have an explanation." "It was between us and the stars," they told him.

The train ran into Chicago. That afternoon there were pictures upside down in the newspapers showing the blue foxes and the yellow flongboos climbing telephone poles standing on their heads eating pink ice cream with iron axes.

Each blue fox and yellow flongboo got a newspaper for himself and each one looked long and careful upside down to see how he looked in the picture in the newspaper climbing a telephone pole standing on his head eating pink ice cream with an iron ax.

Crossing Minnesota the sky began to fill with the snow ghosts of Minnesota snow weather. Again the foxes and flongboos lifted the roof off the car, telling the conductor they would rather wreck the train than miss the big show of the snow ghosts of the first Minnesota snow weather of the winter.

Some went to sleep, but the two baby blue foxes stayed up all night watching the snow ghosts and telling snow ghost stories to each other.

Early in the night the first baby blue fox said to the second, "Who are the snow ghosts the ghosts of?" The second baby blue fox answered, "Everybody who makes a snowball, a snow man, a snow fox or a snow fish or a snow pattycake, everybody has a snow ghost."

And that was only the beginning of their talk. It would take a big book to tell all that the two baby foxes told each other that night about the

Minnesota snow ghosts, because they sat up all night telling old stories their fathers and mothers and grandfathers and grandmothers told them, and making up new stories never heard before about where the snow ghosts go on Christmas morning and how the snow ghosts watch the New Year in.

Somewhere between Winnipeg and Moose Jaw, somewhere it was they stopped the train and all ran out in the snow where the white moon was shining down a valley of birch trees. It was the Snowbird Valley where all the snowbirds of Canada come early in the winter and make their snow shoes.

At last they came to Medicine Hat, near the Saskatchewan River, where the blizzards and the chinooks begin, where nobody works unless they have to and they nearly all have to. There they ran in the snow till they came to the place where the Head Spotter of the Weather Makers sits on a high stool in a high tower on a high hill watching the weather.

"Let loose another big wind to blow back our tails to us, let loose a big freeze to freeze our tails onto us again, and so let us get back our lost tails," they said to the Head Spotter of the Weather Makers.

Which was just what he did, giving them exactly what they wanted, so they all went back home satisfied, the blue foxes each with a big wavy brush of a tail to help him when he runs, when he eats, when he walks or talks, when he makes pictures or writes letters in the snow or when he puts a snack of bacon meat with stripes of fat and lean to hide till he wants it under a big rock by the river–and the yellow flongboos each with a long yellow torch of a tail to light up his home in a hollow tree or to light up his way when he sneaks at night on the prairie, sneaking up on the flangwayer, the hipper, or the hangjast.

Rikki-Tikki-Tavi

From *The Jungle Book*

Rudyard Kipling

At the hole where he went in
Red-Eye called to Wrinkle-Skin.

Hear what little Red-Eye saith:
"Nag, come up and dance with death!"

Eye to eye and head to head
(Keep the measure, Nag.)

This shall end when one is dead
(At thy pleasure, Nag.)

Turn for turn and twist for twist
(Run and hide thee, Nag.)

Hah! The hooded Death has missed!
(Woe betide thee, Nag!)

This is the story of the great war that Rikki-tikki-tavi fought single-handed, through the bathrooms of the big bungalow in Segowlie cantonment. Darzee the Tailorbird helped him, and Chuchundra the Muskrat, who never comes out into the middle of the floor, but always creeps round by the wall, gave him advice, but Rikki-tikki did the real fighting.

He was a mongoose, rather like a little cat in his fur and his tail, but quite like a weasel in his head and his habits. His eyes and the end of his restless nose were pink; he could scratch himself any where he pleased with any leg, front or back, that he chose to use; he could fluff up his tail till it looked like a bottlebrush, and his war cry as he scuttled through the long grass was: *Rikk-tikk-tikki-tzkki-tchk!*

One day, a high summer flood washed him out of the burrow where he lived with his father and mother, and carried him kicking and clucking, down a roadside ditch. He found a little wisp of grass floating there, and clung to it till he lost his senses. When he revived, he was lying in the hot sun on the middle of a garden path, very draggled indeed, and a small boy was saying: "Here's a dead mongoose. Let's have a funeral."

"No," said his mother, "let's take him in and dry him. Perhaps he isn't really dead."

They took him into the house, and a big man picked him up between his finger and thumb and said he was not dead but half choked. So they wrapped him in cotton wool, and warmed him over a little fire, and he opened his eyes and sneezed.

"Now," said the big man (he was an Englishman who had just moved into the bungalow), "don't frighten him, and we'll see what he'll do."

It is the hardest thing in the world to frighten a mongoose because he is eaten up from nose to tail with curiosity. The motto of all the mongoose family is "Run and find out," and Rikki-tikki was a true mongoose. He looked at the cotton wool, decided that it was not good to eat, ran all round the table, sat up and put his fur in order, scratched himself, and jumped on the small boy's shoulder.

"Don't be frightened, Teddy," said his father. "That's his way of making friends."

"Ouch! He's tickling under my chin," said Teddy.

Rikki-tikki looked down between the boy's collar and neck, snuffed at his ear, and climbed down to the floor, where he sat rubbing his nose.

"Good gracious," said Teddy's mother, "and that's a wild creature! I suppose he's so tame because we've been kind to him."

"All mongooses are like that," said her husband. "If Teddy doesn't pick him up by the tail, or try to put him in a cage, he'll run in and out of the house all day long. Let's give him something to eat."

They gave him a little piece of raw meat. Rikki-tikki liked it immensely, and when it was finished he went out into the veranda and sat in the sunshine and fluffed up his fur to make it dry to the roots. Then he felt better.

"There are more things to find out about in this house," he said to himself, "than all my family could find out in all their lives. I shall certainly stay and find out."

He spent all that day roaming over the house. He nearly drowned himself in the bathtubs, put his nose into the ink on a writing table, and burnt it on the end of the big man's cigar, for he climbed up in the big man's lap to see how writing was done. At nightfall he ran into Teddy's nursery to watch how kerosene lamps were lighted, and when Teddy went to bed Rikki-tikki climbed up too. But he was a restless companion, because he had to get up and attend to every noise all through the night, and find out what made it. Teddy's mother and father came in, the last thing, to look at their boy, and Rikki-tikki was awake on the pillow. "I don't like that," said Teddy's mother. "He may bite the child."

"He'll do no such thing," said the father. "Teddy's safer with that little beast than if he had a bloodhound to watch him. If a snake came into the nursery now–"

But Teddy's mother wouldn't think of anything so awful.

Early in the morning Rikki-tikki came to early breakfast in the veranda riding on Teddy's shoulder, and they gave him banana and some boiled egg; and he sat on all their laps one after the other, because every well-brought-up mongoose always hopes to be a house-mongoose some day and have rooms to run about in; and Rikki-tikki's mother (she used to live in the General's house at Segowlie) had carefully told Rikki what to do if ever he came across white men.

Then Rikki-tikki went out into the garden to see what was to be seen. It was a large garden, only half cultivated, with bushes, as big as summerhouses, of Marshal Niel roses, lime and orange trees, clumps of bamboos, and thickets of high grass. Rikki-tikki licked his lips. "This is a splendid hunting ground," he said, and his tail grew bottlebrushy at the thought of it, and he scuttled up and down the garden, snuffing here and there till he heard very sorrowful voices in a thornbush. It was Darzee the Tailorbird and his wife. They had made a beautiful nest by pulling two big leaves together and stitching them up the edges with fibers, and had filled the hollow with cotton and downy fluff. The nest swayed to and fro, as they sat on the rim and cried.

"What is the matter?" asked Rikki-tikki.

"We are very miserable," said Darzee. "One of our babies fell out of the nest yesterday and Nag ate him."

"H'mm!" said Rikki-tikki, "that is very sad—but I am a stranger here. Who is Nag?"

Darzee and his wife only cowered down in the nest without answering, for from the thick grass at the foot of the bush there came a low hiss—a horrid cold sound that made Rikki-tikki jump back two clear feet. Then inch by inch out of the grass rose up the head and spread hood of Nag, the big black cobra, and he was five feet long from tongue to tail. When he had lifted one-third of himself clear of the ground, he stayed balancing to and fro exactly as a dandelion tuft balances in the wind, and he looked at Rikki-tikki with the wicked snake's eyes that never change their expression, whatever the snake may be thinking of.

"Who is Nag?" said he. "*I* am Nag. The great god Brahm put his mark upon all our people, when the first cobra spread his hood to keep the sun off Brahm as he slept. Look, and be afraid!"

He spread out his hood more than ever, and Rikki-tikki saw the spectacle mark on the back of it that looks exactly like the eye part of a hook-and-eye fastening. He was afraid for the minute, but it is impossible for a mongoose to stay frightened for any length of time, and though Rikki-tikki had never met a live cobra before, his mother had fed him on dead ones, and he knew that all a grown mongoose's business in life was to fight and eat snakes. Nag knew that too and, at the bottom of his cold heart, he was afraid.

"Well," said Rikki-tikki, and his tail began to fluff up again, "marks or no marks, do you think it is right for you to eat fledglings out of a nest?"

Nag was thinking to himself, and watching the least little movement in the grass behind Rikki-tikki. He knew that mongooses in the garden meant death sooner or later for him and his family, but he wanted to get Rikki-tikki off his guard. So he dropped his head a little, and put it on one side.

"Let us talk," he said. "You eat eggs. Why should not I eat birds?"

"Behind you! Look behind you!" sang Darzee.

Rikki-tikki knew better than to waste time in staring. He jumped up in the air as high as he could go, and just under him whizzed by the head of Nagaina, Nag's wicked wife. She had crept up behind him as he was talking, to make an end of him, and he heard her savage hiss as the stroke missed. He came down almost across her back, and if he had been an old mongoose he would have known that then was the time to break her back with one bite, but he was afraid of the terrible lashing return stroke of the cobra. He bit, indeed, but did not bite long enough, and he jumped clear of the whisking tail, leaving Nagaina torn and angry.

"Wicked, wicked Darzee!" said Nag, lashing up as high as he could reach towards the nest in the thornbush, but Darzee had built it out of reach of snakes, and it only swayed to and fro.

Rikki-tikki felt his eyes growing red and hot (when a mongoose's eyes grow red, he is angry), and he sat back on his tail and hind legs like a little kangaroo, and looked all round him, and chattered with rage. But Nag and Nagaina had disappeared into the grass. When a snake misses its stroke, it never says anything or gives any sign of what it means to do next. Rikki-tikki did not care to follow them, for he did not feel sure that he could manage two snakes at once. So he trotted off to the gravel path near the house, and sat down to think. It was a serious matter for him. If you read the old books of natural history, you will find they say that when the mongoose fights the snake and happens to get bitten, he runs off and eats some herb that cures him. That is not true. The victory is only a matter of quickness of eye and quickness of foot–snake's blow against mongoose's jump–and as no eye can follow the motion of a snake's head when it strikes, this makes things much more wonderful than any magic herb. Rikki-tikki knew he was a young mongoose, and it made him all the more pleased to think that he had managed to escape a blow from behind. It gave him confidence in himself, and when Teddy came running down the path, Rikki-tikki was ready to be petted. But just as Teddy was stooping, something wriggled a little in the dust, and a tiny voice said: "Be careful. I am Death." It was Karait, the dusty brown snakeling that lies for choice on the dusty earth, and his bite is as dangerous as the cobra's. But he is so small that nobody thinks of him, and so he does the more harm to people.

Rikki-tikki's eyes grew red again, and he danced up to Karait with the peculiar rocking, swaying motion that he had inherited from his family. It looks very funny, but it is so perfectly balanced a gait that you can fly off from it at any angle you please, and in dealing with snakes this is an advantage. If Rikki-tikki had only known, he was doing a much more dangerous thing than fighting Nag, for Karait is so small, and can turn so quickly, that unless Rikki bit him close to the back of the head, he would get the return stroke in his eye or his lip. But Rikki did not know. His eyes were all red, and he rocked back and forth, looking for a good place to hold. Karait struck out, Rikki jumped sideways and tried to run in, but the wicked little dusty gray head lashed within a fraction of his shoulder, and he had to jump over the body, and the head followed his heels close.

Teddy shouted to the house: "Oh, look here! Our mongoose is killing a snake." And Rikki-tikki heard a scream from Teddy's mother. His father ran out with a stick, but by the time he came up, Karait had lunged out once too far, and Rikki-tikki had sprung, jumped on the snake's back, dropped his head far between his forelegs, bitten as high up the back as he could get hold, and rolled away. That bite paralyzed Karait, and Rikki-tikki was just going to eat him up from the tail, after the custom of his family at dinner, when he remembered that a full meal makes a slow mongoose, and if he wanted all his strength and quickness ready, he must keep himself thin. He went away for a dust bath under the castor-oil bushes, while Teddy's father beat the dead Karait. "What is the use of that?" thought Rikki-tikki. "I have settled it all." And then Teddy's mother picked him up from the dust and hugged him, crying that he had saved Teddy from death, and Teddy's father said that he was a providence, and Teddy looked on with big scared eyes. Rikki-tikki was rather amused at all the fuss, which, of course, he did not understand. Teddy's mother might just as well have petted Teddy for playing in the dust. Rikki was thoroughly enjoying himself.

That night at dinner, walking to and fro among the wineglasses on the table, he might have stuffed himself three times over with nice things. But he remembered Nag and Nagaina, and though it was very pleasant to be patted and petted by Teddy's mother and to sit on Teddy's shoulder, his eyes would get red from time to time, and he would go off into his long war cry of *"Rikk-tikk-tikki-tikki-tchk!"*

Teddy carried him off to bed, and insisted on Rikki-tikki sleeping under his chin. Rikki-tikki was too well bred to bite or scratch but as soon as Teddy was asleep he went off for his nightly walk round the house, and in the dark he ran up against Chuchundra the Muskrat creeping round by the wall. Chuchundra is a broken-hearted little beast. He whimpers and cheeps all the night trying to make up his mind to run into the middle of the room, but he never gets there.

"Don't kill me," said Chuchundra, almost weeping. "Rikki-tikki, don't kill me!"

"Do you think a snake-killer kills muskrats?" said Rikki-tikki scornfully.

"Those who kill snakes get killed by snakes," said Chuchundra more sorrowfully than ever. "And how am I to be sure that Nag won't mistake me for you some dark night?"

"There's not the least danger," said Rikki-tikki, "but Nag is in the garden, and I know you don't go there."

"My cousin Chua the Rat told me—" said Chuchundra and then he stopped.

"Told you what?"

"Hsh! Nag is everywhere, Rikki-tikki. You should have talked to Chua in the garden."

"I didn't–so you must tell me. Quick, Chuchundra, or I'll bite you!"

Chuchundra sat down and cried till the tears rolled off his whiskers. "I am a very poor man," he sobbed. "I never had spirit enough to run out into the middle of the room. *Hsh!* I mustn't tell you anything. Can't you *hear,* Rikki-tikki?"

Rikki-tikki listened. The house was as still as still, but he thought he could just catch the faintest *scratch-scratch* in the world–a noise as faint as that of a wasp walking on a window-pane–the dry scratch of a snake's scales on brickwork.

"That's Nag or Nagaina," he said to himself, "and he is crawling into the bathroom sluice. You're right, Chuchundra. I should have talked to Chua."

He stole off to Teddy's bathroom, but there was nothing there, and then to Teddy's mother's bathroom. At the bottom of the smooth plaster wall there was a brick pulled out to make a sluice for the bathwater, and as Rikki-tikki stole in by the masonry curb where the bath is put, he heard Nag and Nagaina whispering together outside in the moonlight.

"When the house is emptied of people," said Nagaina to her husband, "*he* will have to go away, and then the garden will be our own again. Go in quietly, and remember that the big man who killed Karait is the first one to bite. Then come out and tell me, and we will hunt for Rikki-tikki together."

"But are you sure that there is anything to be gained by killing the people?" said Nag.

"Everything. When there were no people in the bungalow, did we have any mongoose in the garden? So long as the bungalow is empty, we are king and queen of the garden. And remember that as soon as our eggs in the melon bed hatch (as they may tomorrow), our children will need room and quiet."

"I had not thought of that," said Nag. "I will go, but there is no need that we should hunt for Rikki-tikki afterwards. I will kill the big man and his wife, and the child if I can, and come away quietly. Then the bungalow will be empty, and Rikki-tikki will go."

Rikki-tikki tingled all over with rage and hatred at this, and then Nag's head came through the sluice, and his five feet of cold body followed it. Angry as he was, Rikki-tikki was very frightened as he saw the size of the big cobra. Nag coiled himself up, raised his head, and looked into the bathroom in the dark, and Rikki could see his eyes glitter.

"Now, if I kill him here, Nagaina will know, and if I fight him on the open floor, the odds are in his favor. What am I to do?" said Rikki-tikki-tavi.

Nag waved to and fro, and then Rikki-tikki heard him drinking from the biggest water jar that was used to fill the bath. "That is good," said the snake. "Now, when Karait was killed, the big man had a stick. He may have that stick still, but when he comes in to bathe in the morning he will not have a stick. I shall wait here till he comes. Nagaina–do you hear me?–I shall wait here in the cool till daytime."

There was no answer from outside, so Rikki-tikki knew Nagaina had gone away. Nag coiled himself down, coil by coil, round the bulge at the bottom of the water jar, and Rikki-tikki stayed still as death. After an hour he began to move, muscle by muscle, towards the jar. Nag was asleep, and Rikki-tikki looked at his big back, wondering which would be the best place for a good hold. "If I don't break his back at the first jump," said Rikki, "he can still fight, and if he fights–O Rikki!" He looked at the thickness of the neck below the hood, but that was too much for him, and a bite near the tail would only make Nag savage.

"It must be the head," he said at last, "the head above the hood. And, when I am once there, I must not let go."

Then he jumped. The head was lying a little clear of the water jar, under the curve of it, and, as his teeth met, Rikki braced his back against the bulge of the red earthenware to hold down the head. This gave him just one second's purchase, and he made the most of it. Then he was battered to and fro as a rat is shaken by a dog–to and fro on the floor, up and down, and round in great circles, but his eyes were red and he held on as the body cart-wheeled over the floor, upsetting the tin dipper and the soap dish and the flesh brush, and banged against the tin side of the bath. As he held he closed his jaws tighter and tighter, for he made sure he would be banged to death, and, for the honor of his family, he preferred to be found with his teeth locked. He was dizzy, aching, and felt shaken to pieces when something went off like a thunderclap just behind him; a hot wind knocked him senseless and red fire singed his fur. The big man had been wakened by the noise, and had fired both barrels of a shotgun into Nag just behind the hood.

Rikki-tikki held on with his eyes shut, for now he was quite sure he was dead, but the head did not move, and the big man picked him up and said: "It's the mongoose again, Alice. The little chap has saved *our* lives now." Then Teddy's mother came in with a very white face, and saw what was left of Nag, and Rikki-tikki dragged himself to Teddy's bedroom and spent half the rest of the night shaking himself tenderly to find out whether he really was broken into forty pieces, as he fancied.

When morning came he was very stiff, but well pleased with his doings: "Now I have Nagaina to settle with, and she will be worse than five Nags, and there's no knowing when the eggs she spoke of will hatch. Goodness! I must go and see Darzee," he said.

Without waiting for breakfast, Rikki-tikki ran to the thornbush where Darzee was singing a song of triumph at the top of his voice. The news of Nag's death was all over the garden, for the sweeper had thrown the body on the rubbish heap.

"Oh, you stupid tuft of feathers!" said Rikki-tikki angrily. "Is this the time to sing?"

"Nag is dead–is dead–is dead!" sang Darzee. "The valiant Rikki-tikki caught him by the head and held fast. The big man brought the bangstick, and Nag fell in two pieces! He will never eat my babies again."

"All that's true enough, but where's Nagaina?" said Rikki-tikki, looking carefully round him.

"Nagaina came to the bathroom sluice and called for Nag," Darzee went on, "and Nag came out on the end of a stick–the sweeper picked him up on the end of a stick and threw him upon the rubbish heap. Let us sing about the great, the red-eyed Rikki-tikki!" And Darzee filled his throat and sang.

"If I could get up to your nest, I'd roll your babies out!" said Rikki-tikki. "You don't know when to do the right thing at the right time. You're safe enough in your nest there, but it's war for me down here. Stop singing a minute, Darzee."

"For the great, the beautiful Rikki-tikki's sake I will stop," said Darzee. "What is it, O killer of the terrible Nag?"

"Where is Nagaina, for the third time?"

"On the rubbish heap by the stables, mourning for Nag. Great is Rikki-tikki with the white teeth."

"Bother my white teeth! Have you ever heard where she keeps her eggs?"

"In the melon bed, on the end nearest the wall, where the sun strikes nearly all day. She hid them there weeks ago."

"And you never thought it worthwhile to tell me? The end nearest the wall, you said?"

"Rikki-tikki, you are not going to eat her eggs?"

"Not eat exactly–no. Darzee, if you have a grain of sense you will fly off to the stables and pretend that your wing is broken, and let Nagaina chase you away to this bush. I must get to the melon bed, and if I went there now she'd see me."

Darzee was a featherbrained little fellow who could never hold more than one idea at a time in his head, and just because he knew that Nagaina's children were born in eggs like his own, he didn't think at first that it was fair to kill them. But his wife was a sensible bird, and she knew that cobra's eggs meant young cobras later on. So she flew off from the nest, and left Darzee to keep the babies warm, and continue his song about the death of Nag. Darzee was very like a man in some ways.

She fluttered in front of Nagaina by the rubbish heap, and cried out: "Oh, my wing is broken! The boy in the house threw a stone at me and broke it." Then she fluttered more desperately than ever.

Nagaina lifted up her head and hissed: "You warned Rikki-tikki when I would have killed him. Indeed and truly, you've chosen a bad place to be lame in." And she moved towards Darzee's wife, slipping along over the dust.

"The boy broke it with a stone!" shrieked Darzee's wife.

"Well! It may be some consolation to you when you're dead to know that I shall settle accounts with the boy. My husband lies on the rubbish heap this morning, but before night the boy in the house will lie very still. What is the use of running away? I am sure to catch you. Little fool, look at me!"

Darzee's wife knew better than to do *that,* for a bird who looks at a snake's eyes gets so frightened that she cannot move. Darzee's wife fluttered on, piping sorrowfully, and never leaving the ground, and Nagaina quickened her pace.

Rikki-tikki heard them going up the path from the stables, and he raced for the end of the melon patch near the wall. There, in the warm litter above the melons, very cunningly hidden, he found twenty-five eggs, about the size of a bantam's eggs, but with whitish skins instead of shells.

"I was not a day too soon," he said, for he could see the baby cobras curled up inside the skin, and he knew that the minute they were hatched they could each kill a man or a mongoose. He bit off the tops of the eggs as fast as he could, taking care to crush the young cobras, and turned over the litter from time to time to see whether he had missed any. At last there were only three eggs left, and Rikki-tikki began to chuckle to himself, when he heard Darzee's wife screaming:

"Rikki-tikki, I led Nagaina towards the house, and she has gone into the veranda, and–oh, come quickly–she means killing!"

Rikki-tikki smashed two eggs, and tumbled backwards down the melon bed with the third egg in his mouth, and scuttled to the veranda as hard as he could put foot to the ground. Teddy and his mother and father were there at early breakfast, but Rikki-tikki saw that they were not eating anything. They sat stone-still, and their faces were white. Nagaina was coiled up on the matting by Teddy's chair, within easy striking distance of Teddy's bare leg, and she was swaying to and fro, singing a song of triumph.

"Son of the big man that killed Nag," she hissed, "stay still. I am not ready yet. Wait a little. Keep very still, all you three! If you move I strike, and if you do not move I strike. Oh, foolish people, who killed my Nag!"

Teddy's eyes were fixed on his father, and all his father could do was to whisper: "Sit still, Teddy. You mustn't move. Teddy, keep still."

Then Rikki-tikki came up and cried: "Turn round, Nagaina, turn and fight!"

"All in good time," said she, without moving her eyes. "I will settle my account with *you* presently. Look at your friends, Rikki-tikki. They are still and white. They are afraid. They dare not move, and if you come a step nearer I strike."

"Look at your eggs," said Rikki-tikki, "in the melon bed near the wall. Go and look, Nagaina!"

The big snake turned half round, and saw the egg on the veranda. "Ah-h! Give it to me," she said.

Rikki-tikki put his paws one on each side of the egg, and his eyes were blood red. "What price for a snake's egg? For a young cobra? For a young king-cobra? For the last–the very last of the brood? The ants are eating all the others down by the melon bed."

Nagaina spun clear round, forgetting everything for the sake of the one egg, and Rikki-tikki saw Teddy's father shoot out a big hand, catch Teddy by the shoulder, and drag him across the little table with the teacups, safe and out of reach of Nagaina.

"Tricked! Tricked! Tricked! *Rikk-tck-tck!*" chuckled Rikki-tikki. "The boy is safe, and it was I–I–I that caught Nag by the hood last night in the bathroom." Then he began to jump up and down, all four feet together, his head close to the floor. "He threw me to and fro, but he could not shake me off. He was dead before the big man blew him in two. I did it! *Rikki-tikki-tck-tck!* Come then, Nagaina. Come and fight with me. You shall not be a widow long."

Nagaina saw that she had lost her chance of killing Teddy, and the egg lay between Rikki-tikki's paws. "Give me the egg, Rikki-tikki. Give me the last of my eggs, and I will go away and never come back," she said, lowering her hood.

"Yes, you will go away, and you will never come back, for you will go to the rubbish heap with Nag. Fight, widow! The big man has gone for his gun! Fight!"

Rikki-tikki was bounding all round Nagaina, keeping just out of reach of her stroke, his little eyes like hot coals. Nagaina gathered herself together, and flung out at him. Rikki-tikki jumped up and backwards. Again and again and again she struck, and each time her head came with a whack on the matting of the veranda and she gathered herself together like a watch spring.

Then Rikki-tikki danced in a circle to get behind her, and Nagaina spun round to keep her head to his head, so that the rustle of her tail on the matting sounded like dry leaves blown along by the wind.

He had forgotten the egg. It still lay on the veranda, and Nagaina came nearer and nearer to it, till at last, while Rikki-tikki was drawing breath, she caught it in her mouth, turned to the veranda steps, and flew like an arrow down the path, with Rikki-tikki behind her. When the cobra runs for her life, she goes like a whiplash flicked across a horse's neck. Rikki-tikki knew that he must catch her, or all the trouble would begin again. She headed straight for the long grass by the thornbush, and as he was running Rikki-tikki heard Darzee still singing his foolish little song of triumph. But Darzee's wife was wiser. She flew off her nest as Nagaina came along, and flapped her wings about Nagaina's head. If Darzee had helped they might have turned her, but Nagaina only lowered her hood and went on. Still, the instant's delay brought Rikki-tikki up to her, and as she plunged into the rat hole where she and Nag used to live, his little white teeth were clenched on her tail, and he went down with her–and very few mongooses, however wise and old they may be, care to follow a cobra into its hole. It was dark in the hole, and Rikki-tikki never knew when it might open out and give Nagaina room to turn and strike at him. He held on savagely, and stuck out his feet to act as brakes on the dark slope of the hot, moist earth. Then the grass by the mouth of the hole stopped waving, and Darzee said: "It is all over with Rikki-tikki! We must sing his death song. Valiant Rikki-tikki is dead! For Nagaina will surely kill him underground."

So he sang a very mournful song that he made up on the spur of the minute, and just as he got to the most touching part the grass quivered again, and Rikki-tikki, covered with dirt, dragged himself out of the hole leg by leg, licking his whiskers. Darzee stopped with a little shout. Rikki-tikki shook some of the dust out of his fur and sneezed. "It is all over," he said. "The widow will never come out again." And the red ants that live between the grass stems heard him, and began to troop down one after another to see if he had spoken the truth.

Rikki-tikki curled himself up in the grass and slept where he was–slept and slept till it was late in the afternoon, for he had done a hard day's work.

"Now," he said, when he awoke, "I will go back to the house. Tell the coppersmith, Darzee, and he will tell the garden that Nagaina is dead."

The coppersmith is a bird who makes a noise exactly like the beating of a little hammer on a copper pot, and the reason he is always making it is because he is the town crier to every Indian garden, and tells all the news to everybody who cares to listen. As Rikki-tikki went up the path, he heard his "attention" notes like a tiny dinner gong, and then the steady *"Ding-dong-tock!* Nag is dead–*dong!* Nagaina is dead! *Ding-dong-tock!"* That set all the birds in the garden singing, and the frogs croaking, for Nag and Nagaina used to eat frogs as well as little birds.

When Rikki got to the house, Teddy and Teddy's mother (she looked very white still, for she had been fainting) and Teddy's father came out and almost cried over him. And that night he ate all that was given him till he could eat no more, and went to bed on Teddy's shoulder, where Teddy's mother saw him when she came to look late at night.

"He saved our lives and Teddy's life," she said to her husband.

"Just think, he saved all our lives."

Rikki-tikki woke up with a jump, for the mongooses are light sleepers.

"Oh, it's you," said he. "What are you bothering for? All the cobras are dead, and if they weren't, I'm here."

Rikki-tikki had a right to be proud of himself. But he did not grow too proud, and he kept that garden as a mongoose should keep it, with tooth and jump and spring and bite, till never a cobra dared show its head inside the walls.

The Butterfly's Ball

William Roscoe

"Come, take up your hats, and away let us haste
To the Butterfly's Ball and the Grasshoppers Feast;
The trumpeter, Gadfly, has summoned the crew,
And the revels are now only waiting for you."

So said little Robert, and pacing along,
His merry companions came forth in a throng,
And on the smooth grass by the side of a wood,
Beneath a broad oak that for ages has stood,
Saw the children of earth and the tenants of air
For an evening's amusement together repair.

And there came the Beetle, so blind and so black,
Who carried the Emmet, his friend, on his back;
And there was the Gnat and the Dragonfly too,
With all their relations, green, orange, and blue.

And there came the Moth, with his plumage of down,
And the Hornet, in jacket of yellow and brown,
Who with him the Wasp, his companion, did bring:
They promised that evening to lay by their sting.

And the sly little Dormouse crept out of his hole,
And brought to the Feast his blind brother, the Mole.
And the Snail, with his horns peeping out of his shell,
Came from a great distance–the length of an ell.

A mushroom their table, and on it was laid
A water-dock leaf, which a tablecloth made.
The viands were various, to each of their taste,
And the Bee brought her honey to crown the repast.

Then close on his haunches, so solemn and wise,
The Frog from a corner looked up to the skies;
And the Squirrel, well-pleased such diversions to see,
Mounted high overhead and looked down from a tree.

Then out came a Spider, with fingers so fine,
To show his dexterity on the tight line.
From one branch to another his cobwebs he slung,
Then quick as an arrow he darted along.

But just in the middle–oh! shocking to tell,
From his rope, in an instant, poor Harlequin fell.
Yet he touched not the ground, but with talons outspread,
Hung suspended in air, at the end of a thread.

Then the Grasshopper came, with a jerk and a spring,
Very long was his leg, though but short was his wing;
He took but three leaps, and was soon out of sight,
Then chirped his own praises the rest of the night.

With step so majestic, the Snail did advance,
And promised the gazers a minuet to dance:
But they all laughed so loud that he pulled in his head,
And went to his own little chamber to bed.
Then as evening gave way to the shadows of night,
Their watchman, the Glow-worm, came out with a light.

"Then home let us hasten while yet we can see,
For no watchman is waiting for you and for me."
So said little Robert, and pacing along,
His merry companions returned in a throng.

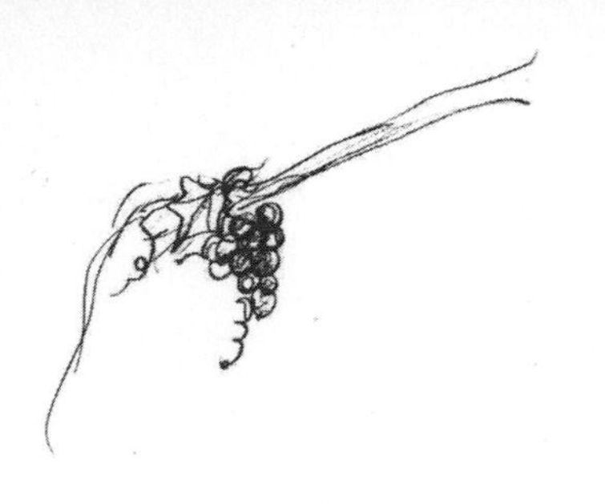

The Fox and the Grapes

Aesop

One hot summer day a Fox was strolling through an orchard until he came to a bunch of grapes just ripening on a vine which had been trained to grow over a lofty branch.

"Just the things to quench my thirst," said he. Drawing back a few paces, he took a run and a jump, and just missed the bunch. Turning round again with a One, Two, Three, he jumped up, but with no greater success. Again and again he tried for the tempting morsel, but at last had to give it up, and walked away with his nose in the air, saying: "I am sure they are sour."

"It is easy to despise what you cannot get."

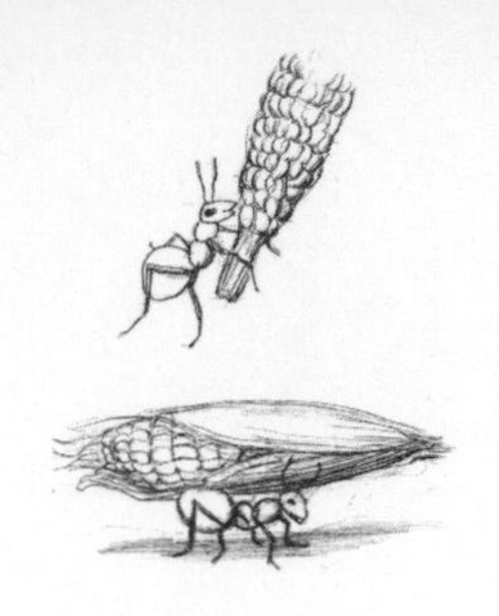

THE ANT AND THE GRASSHOPPER

AESOP

In a field one summer's day a Grasshopper was hopping about, chirping and singing to its heart's content. An Ant passed by, bearing along with great effort an ear of corn he was taking to the nest.

"Why not come and chat with me," said the Grasshopper, "instead of toiling and straining in that way?"

"I am helping to lay up food for the winter," said the Ant, "and recommend you do the same."

"Why bother about winter?" said the Grasshopper; "we have got plenty of food at present."

But the Ant went on its way and continued its toil. When the winter came the Grasshopper had no food, and found itself dying of hunger, while every day it saw the ants distributing corn and grain from the stores they had collected in the summer. Then the Grasshopper knew:

"It is best to prepare for the days of necessity."

THE GARDEN OF DREAMS AND THE PRIVATE ZOO

FROM *THE VOYAGES OF DOCTOR DOLITTLE*

HUGH LOFTING

When breakfast was over the Doctor took me out to show me the garden. Well, if the house had been interesting, the garden was a hundred times more so. Of all the gardens I have ever seen that was the most delightful, the most fascinating. At first you did not realize how big it was. You never seemed to come to the end of it. When at last you were quite sure that you had seen it all, you would peer over a hedge, or turn a corner, or look up some steps, and there was a whole new part you never expected to find.

It had everything–everything a garden can have, or ever has had. There were wide, wide lawns with carved stone seats, green with moss. Over the lawns hung weeping willows, and their feathery bough tips brushed the velvet grass when they swung with the wind. The old flagged paths had high, clipped yew hedges either side of them, so that they looked like the narrow streets of some old town; and through the hedges, doorways had been made; and over the doorways were shapes like vases and peacocks and half-moons all trimmed out of the living trees. There was a lovely marble fishpond with golden carp and blue water lilies in it and big green frogs. A high brick wall alongside the kitchen garden was all covered with pink-and-yellow peaches ripening in the sun. There was a wonderful great oak, hollow in the trunk, big enough for four men to hide inside. Many summerhouses there were, too–some of wood and some of stone, and one of them was full of books to read. In a corner, among some rocks and ferns, was an outdoor fireplace, where the Doctor used to fry liver and bacon when he had a notion to take his meals in the open air. There was a couch as well on which he used to sleep, it seems, on warm summer nights when the nightingales were singing at their best; it had wheels on it so it could be moved about under any tree they sang in. But the thing that fascinated me most of all was a tiny little tree house, high up in the top branches of a great elm, with a long rope ladder leading to it. The Doctor told me he used it for looking at the moon and the stars through a telescope.

It was the kind of a garden where you could wander and explore for days and days–always coming upon something new, always glad to find the old spots over again. That first time that I saw the Doctor's garden I was so charmed by it that I felt I would like to live in it–always and always–and never go outside of it again. For it had everything within its walls to give happiness, to make living pleasant–to keep the heart at peace. It was the Garden of Dreams.

One peculiar thing I noticed immediately when I came into it, and that was what a lot of birds there were about. Every tree seemed to have two or three nests in it. And heaps of other wild creatures appeared to be making themselves at home there, too. Stoats and tortoises and dormice seemed to be quite common, and not in the least shy. Toads of different colors and sizes hopped about the lawn as though it belonged to them. Green lizards (which were very rare in Puddleby) sat up on the stones in the sunlight and blinked at us. Even snakes were to be seen.

"You need not be afraid of them," said the Doctor, noticing that I started somewhat when a large black snake wiggled across the path right in front of us. "These fellows are not poisonous. They do a great deal of good in keeping down many kinds of garden pests. I play the flute to them sometimes in the evening. They love it. Stand right up on their tails and carry on no end. Funny thing, their taste for music."

"Why do all these animals come and live here?" I asked. "I never saw a garden with so many creatures in it."

"Well, I suppose it's because they get the kind of food they like, and nobody worries or disturbs them. And then, of course, they know me. And if they or their children get sick I presume they find it handy to be living in a doctor's garden–Look! You see that sparrow on the sundial, swearing at the blackbird down below? Well, he has been coming here every summer for years. He comes from London. The country sparrows round about here are always laughing at him. They say he chirps with such a Cockney accent. He is a most amusing bird–very brave but very cheeky. He loves nothing better than an argument, but he always ends it by getting rude. He is a real city bird. In London he lives around St. Paul's Cathedral. 'Cheapside,' we call him."

"Are all these birds from the country round here?" I asked.

"Most of them," said the Doctor. "But a few rare ones visit me every year who ordinarily never come near England at all. For instance, that handsome little fellow hovering over the snapdragon there, he's a ruby-throated hummingbird. Comes from America. Strictly speaking, he has no business in this climate at all. It is too cool. I make him sleep in the kitchen at night. Then every August, about the last week of the month, I have a purple bird-of-paradise come all the way from Brazil to see me. She is a very great swell. Hasn't arrived yet of course. And there are a few others, foreign birds from the tropics mostly, who drop in on me in the course of the summer months. But come, I must show you the zoo."

I did not think there could be anything left in that garden which we had not seen. But the Doctor took me by the arm and started off down a little narrow path and after many windings and twistings and turnings we found ourselves before a small door in the high stone wall. The Doctor pushed it open.

Inside was still another garden. I had expected to find cages with animals inside them. But there were none to be seen. Instead there were little stone houses here and there all over the garden, and each house had a window and a door. As we walked in, many of these doors opened and animals came running out to us evidently expecting food.

"Haven't the doors any locks on them?" I asked the Doctor.

"Oh yes," he said. "Every door has a lock. But in my zoo the doors open from the inside, not from the out. The locks are only there so the animals can go and shut themselves in anytime they want to get away from the annoyance of other animals or from people who might come here. Every animal in the zoo stays here because he likes it, not because he is made to."

"They all look very happy and clean," I said. "Would you mind telling me the names of some of them?"

"Certainly. Well now, that funny-looking thing with plates on his back, nosing under the brick over there, is a South American armadillo. The little chap talking to him is a Canadian woodchuck. They both live in those holes you see at the foot of the wall. The two little beats doing antics in the pond are a pair of Russian minks–and that reminds me: I must go and get them some herrings from the town before noon–it is early-closing today. That animal just stepping out of his house is an antelope, one of the smaller South African kinds. Now let us move to the other side of those bushes there and I will show you some more."

"Are those deer over there?" I asked.

"Deer!" said the Doctor. "Where do you mean?"

"Over there," I said, pointing, "nibbling the grass border of the bed. There are two of them."

"Oh, that," said the Doctor with a smile. "That isn't two animals: that's one animal with two heads–the only two-headed animal in the world. It's called the pushmi-pullyu.' I brought him from Africa. He's very tame–acts as a kind of night watchman for my zoo. He only sleeps with one head at a time, you see–very handy–the other head stays awake all night."

"Have you any lions or tigers?" I asked as we moved on.

"No," said the Doctor. "It wouldn't be possible to keep them here–and I wouldn't keep them even if I could. If I had my way, Stubbins, there wouldn't be a single lion or tiger in captivity anywhere in the world. They never take to it. They're never happy. They never settle down. They are always thinking of the big countries they have left behind. You can see it in their eyes, dreaming–dreaming always of the great open spaces where they were born; dreaming of the deep, dark jungles where their mothers first taught them how to scent and track deer. And what are they given in exchange for all this?" asked the Doctor, stopping in his walk and growing all red and angry. "What are they given in exchange for the glory of the African sunrise, for the twilight breeze whispering through the palms, for the green shade of the matted, tangled vines, for the cool, big-starred nights of the desert, for the patter of the waterfall after a hard day's hunt? What, I ask you, are they given in exchange for these? Why, a bare cage with iron bars, an ugly piece of dead meat thrust in to them once a day, and a crowd of fools to come and stare at them with open mouths! No, Stubbins. Lions and tigers, the big hunters, should never, never be seen in zoos."

The Doctor seemed to have grown terribly serious–almost sad. But suddenly his manner changed again and he took me by the arm with his same old cheerful smile.

"But we haven't seen the butterfly houses yet–nor the aquariums. Come along. I am very proud of my butterfly houses."

Off we went again and came presently into a hedged enclosure. Here I saw several big huts made of fine wire netting, like cages. Inside the netting all sorts of beautiful flowers were growing in the sun, with butterflies skimming over them. The Doctor pointed to the end of one of the huts where little boxes with holes in them stood in a row.

"Those are hatching boxes," said he. "There I put the different kinds of caterpillars. And as soon as they turn into butterflies and moths they come out into these flower gardens to feed."

"Do butterflies have a language?" I asked.

"Oh, I fancy they have," said the Doctor, "and the beetles too. But so far I haven't succeeded in learning much about insect languages. I have been too busy lately trying to master the shellfish talk. I mean to take it up, though."

At that moment Polynesia joined us and said, "Doctor, there are two guinea pigs at the back door. They say they have run away from the boy who kept them because they didn't get the right stuff to eat. They want to know if you will take them in."

"All right," said the Doctor. "Show them the way to the zoo. Give them the house on the left, near the gate–the one the black fox had. Tell them what the rules are and give them a square meal. Now, Stubbins, we will go on to the aquariums. And first of all I must show you my big glass seawater tank where I keep the shellfish."

How to Tell Corn Fairies If You See 'Em

Carl Sandburg

If you have ever watched the little corn begin to march across the black lands and then slowly change to big corn and go marching on from the little corn moon of summer to the big corn harvest moon of autumn, then you must have guessed who it is that helps the corn come along. It is the corn fairies. Leave out the corn fairies and there wouldn't be any corn.

All children know this. All boys and girls know that corn is no good unless there are corn fairies.

Have you ever stood in Illinois or Iowa and watched the late summer wind or the early fall wind running across a big cornfield? It looks as if a big, long blanket were being spread out for dancers to come and dance on. If you look close and if you listen close you can see the corn fairies come dancing and singing–sometimes. If it is a wild day and a hot sun is pouring down while a cool north wind blows–and this happens sometimes–then you will be sure to see thousands of corn fairies marching and counter-marching in mocking grand marches over the big, long blanket of green and silver. Then too they sing, only you must listen with your littlest and newest ears if you wish to hear their singing. They sing soft songs that go pla-sizzy pla-sizzy-sizzy, and each song is softer than an eye wink, softer than a Nebraska baby's thumb.

And Spink, who is a little girl living in the same house with the man writing this story, and Skabootch, who is another little girl in the same house–both Spink and Skabootch are asking the question, "How can we tell corn fairies if we see 'em? If we meet a corn fairy how will we know it?" And this is the explanation the man gave to Spink, who is older than Skabootch, and to Skabootch who is younger than Spink:

All corn fairies wear overalls. They work hard, the corn fairies, and they are proud. The reason they are proud is because they work so hard. And the reason they work so hard is because they have overalls.

But understand this. The overalls are corn gold cloth, woven from leaves of ripe corn mixed with ripe October corn silk. In the first week of the harvest moon coming up red and changing to yellow and silver the corn fairies sit by thousands between the corn rows weaving and stitching the clothes they have to wear next winter, next spring, next summer.

They sit cross-legged when they sew. And it is a law among them each one must point the big toe at the moon while sewing the harvest moon clothes. When the moon comes up red as blood early in the evening they point their big toes slanting toward the east. Then towards midnight when the moon is yellow and half way up the sky their big toes are only half slanted as they sit cross-legged sewing. And after midnight when the moon sails its silver disk high overhead and toward the west, then the corn fairies sit sewing with their big toes pointed nearly straight up.

If it is a cool night and looks like frost, then the laughter of the corn fairies is something worth seeing. All the time they sit sewing their next year clothes they are laughing. It is not a law they have to laugh. They laugh because they are half-tickled and glad because it is a good corn year.

And whenever the corn fairies laugh then the laugh comes out of the mouth like a thin gold frost. If you should be lucky enough to see a thousand corn fairies sitting between the corn rows and all of them laughing, you would laugh with wonder yourself to see the gold frost coming from their mouths while they laughed.

Travelers who have traveled far, and seen many things, say that if you know the corn fairies with a real knowledge you can always tell by the stitches in their clothes what state they are from.

In Illinois the corn fairies stitch fifteen stitches of ripe corn silk across the woven corn leaf cloth. In Iowa they stitch sixteen stitches, in Nebraska seventeen, and the farther west you go the more corn silk stitches the corn fairies have in the corn cloth clothes they wear.

In Minnesota one year there were fairies with a blue sash of corn-flowers across their chests. In the Dakotas the same year all the fairies wore pumpkin-flower neckties, yellow four-in-hands, and yellow ascots. And in one strange year it happened in both the states of Ohio and Texas the corn fairies wore little bracelets of white morning glories.

The traveler who heard about this asked many questions and found out the reason why that year the corn fairies wore little bracelets of white morning glories. He said, "Whenever fairies are sad they wear white. And this year, which was long ago, was the year men were tearing down all the old zigzag rail fences. Now those old zigzag rail fences were beautiful for the fairies because a hundred fairies could sit on one rail and thousands and thousands of them could sit on the zigzags and sing pla-sizzy, pla-sizzy-sizzy, softer than an eye-wink, softer than a baby's thumb, all on a moonlit summer night. And they found out that year was going to be the last year of the zigzag rail fences. It made them sorry and sad, and when they are sorry and sad they wear white. So they picked the wonderful white morning glories; running along the zigzag rail fences and made them into little bracelets and wore those bracelets the next year to show they were sorry and sad."

Of course, all this helps you to know how the corn fairies look in the evening, the nighttime, and the moonlight. Now we shall see how they look in the daytime.

In the daytime the corn fairies have their overalls of corn gold cloth on. And they walk among the corn rows and climb the corn stalks and fix things in the leaves and stalks and ears of the corn. They help it to grow.

Each one carries on the left shoulder a mouse brush to brush away the field mice. And over the right shoulder each one has a cricket broom to sweep away the crickets. The brush is a whisk brush to brush away mice that get foolish. And the broom is to sweep away crickets that get foolish.

Around the middle of each corn fairy is a yellow-belly belt. And stuck in this belt is a purple moon shaft hammer. Whenever the wind blows strong and nearly blows the corn down, then the fairies run out and take their purple moon shaft hammers out of their yellow-belly belts and nail down nails to keep the corn from blowing down. When a rainstorm is blowing up terrible and driving all kinds of terribles across the cornfield, then you can be sure of one thing. Running like the wind among the corn rows are the fairies, jerking their purple moon shaft hammers out of their belts and nailing nails down to keep the corn standing up so it will grow and be ripe and beautiful when the harvest moon comes again in the fall.

Spink and Skabootch ask where the corn fairies get the nails. The answer to Spink and Skabootch is, "Next week you will learn all about where the corn fairies get the nails to nail down the corn if you will keep your faces washed and your ears washed till next week."

And the next time you stand watching a big cornfield in late summer or early fall, when the wind is running across the green and silver, listen with your littlest and newest ears. Maybe you will hear the corn fairies going pla-sizzy, pla-sizzy-sizzy, softer than an eye wink, softer than a Nebraska baby's thumb.

Hope Is the Thing With Feathers

Emily Dickinson

Hope is the thing with feathers
That perches in the soul
And sings the tune without the words
And never stops at all,

And sweetest in the gale is heard;
And sore must be the storm
That could abash the little bird
That kept so many warm.

I've heard it in the chillest land
And on the strangest sea,
Yet never, in extremity,
It asked a crumb of me.

My Shadow

Robert Louis Stevenson

I have a little shadow that goes in and out with me,
And what can be the use of him is more than I can see.
He is very, very like me from the heels up to the head;
And I see him jump before me, when I jump into my bed.

The funniest thing about him is the way he likes to grow–
Not at all like proper children, which is always very slow;
For he sometimes shoots up taller, like an india-rubber ball,
And he sometimes gets so little that there's none of him at all.

He hasn't got a notion of how children ought to play,
And can only make a fool of me in every sort of way.
He stays so close beside me, he's a coward you can see;
I'd think shame to stick to nursie as that shadow sticks to me!

One morning, very early, before the sun was up,
I rose and found the shining dew on every buttercup;
But my lazy little shadow, like an arrant sleepyhead,
Had stayed at home behind me and was fast asleep in bed.

The Spider and the Fly

Mary Howitt

"Will you walk into my parlor?" said the Spider to the Fly–
"Tis the prettiest little parlor that ever you did spy;
The way into my parlor is up a winding stair,
And I have many curious things to show you when you're there."

"Oh, no, no," said the little Fly, "to ask me is in vain,
For who goes up your winding stair can ne'er come down again."

"I'm sure you must be weary, dear, with soaring up so high;
Will you rest upon my little bed?" said the Spider to the Fly.
"There are pretty curtains drawn around, the sheets are fine and thin,
And if you like to rest a while, I'll snugly tuck you in!"

"Oh, no, no," said the little Fly, "for I've often heard it said,
They never, never wake again, who sleep upon your bed!"

Said the cunning Spider to the Fly: "Dear friend, what can I do
To prove the warm affection I've always felt for you?
I have, within my pantry, good store of all that's nice;
I'm sure you're very welcome–will you please to take a slice?"

"Oh, no, no," said the little Fly, "kind sir, that cannot be,
I've heard what's in your pantry, and I do not wish to see!"

"Sweet creature," said the Spider, "you're witty and you're wise;
How handsome are your gauzy wings, how brilliant are your eyes!
I have a little looking glass upon my parlor shelf,
If you'll step in one moment, dear, you shall behold yourself."

"I thank you, gentle sir," she said, "for what you're pleased to say,
And bidding you good morning now, I'll call another day."

The Spider turned him round about, and went into his den,
For well he knew the silly Fly would soon come back again;
So he wove a subtle web, in a little corner sly,
And set his table ready, to dine upon the Fly.

Then he came out to his door again, and merrily did sing–
"Come hither, hither, pretty Fly, with the pearl and silver wing;

Your robes are green and purple, there's a crest upon your head;
Your eyes are like the diamond bright, but mine are dull as lead!"

Alas, alas! how very soon this silly little Fly,
Hearing his wily, flattering words, came slowly flitting by:
With buzzing wings she hung aloft, then near and nearer drew–
Thinking only of her crested head–poor foolish thing! At last,
Up jumped the cunning Spider, and fiercely held her fast;
He dragged her up his winding stair, into his dismal den,
Within his little parlor–but she ne'er came out again!

And now, dear little children, who may this story read,
To idle, silly, flattering words, I pray you ne'er give heed:
Unto an evil counselor close heart, and ear, and eye,
And take a lesson from this tale, of the Spider and the Fly.

Paul Revere's Ride

Henry Wadsworth Longfellow

Listen, my children, and you shall hear
Of the midnight ride of Paul Revere.
On the eighteenth of April, in Seventy-five;
Hardly a man is now alive
Who remembers that famous day and year.

He said to his friend, "If the British march
By land or sea from the town tonight,

Hang a lantern aloft in the belfry arch
Of the North Church tower as a signal light–
One, if by land, and two, if by sea;
And I on the opposite shore will be,
Ready to ride and spread the alarm
Through every Middlesex village and farm,
For the country-folk to be up and to arm."

Then he said, "Good night!" and with muffled oar
Silently rowed to the Charles Town shore,
Just as the moon rose over the bay,
Where swinging wide at her moorings lay
The Somerset, British man-of-war;
A phantom ship, with each mast and spar
Across the moon like a prison bar,
And a huge black hulk, that was magnified
By its own reflection in the tide.

Meanwhile, his friend, through alley and street,
Wanders and watches with eager ears,
Till in silence around him he hears
The muster of men at the barrack door,
The sound of arms, and the tramp of feet,

And the measured tread of the grenadiers,
Marching down to their boats on the shore.

Then he climbed to the tower of the church,
Up the wooden stairs, with stealthy tread,
To the belfry-chamber overhead,
And startled the pigeons from their perch
On the somber rafters, that round him made
Masses and moving shapes of shade–
Up the trembling ladder, steep and tall,
To the highest window in the wall,
Where he paused to listen and look down
A moment on the roofs of the town,
And the moonlight flowing over all.

Beneath, in the churchyard, lay the dead,
In their night-encampment on the hill,
Wrapped in silence so deep and still
That he could hear, like a sentinel's tread,
The watchful night-wind, as it went
Creeping along from tent to tent,
And seeming to whisper, "All is well!"
A moment only he feels the spell

Of the place and the hour, and the secret dread
Of the lonely belfry and the dead;
For suddenly all his thoughts are bent
On a shadowy something far away,
Where the river widens to meet the bay–
A line of black that bends and floats
On the rising tide, like a bridge of boats.

Meanwhile, impatient to mount and ride,
Booted and spurred, with a heavy stride
On the opposite shore walked Paul Revere.
Now he patted his horse's side,
Now gazed at the landscape far and near,
Then, impetuous, stamped the earth,
And turned and tightened his saddle-girth;
But mostly he watched with eager search
The belfry-tower of the Old North Church,
As it rose above the graves on the hill,
Lonely and spectral and somber and still.
And lo! as he looks, on the belfry's height
A glimmer, and then a gleam of light!
He springs to the saddle, the bridle he turns,

But lingers and gazes, till full on his sight
A second lamp in the belfry burns!

A hurry of hoofs in a village street,
A shape in the moonlight, a bulk in the dark,
And beneath, from the pebbles, in passing, a spark
Struck out by a steed flying fearless and fleet;
That was all! And yet, through the gloom and the light,
The fate of a nation was riding that night;
And the spark struck out by that steed, in his flight,
Kindled the land into flame with its heat.

He has left the village and mounted the steep,
And beneath him, tranquil and broad and deep,
Is the Mystic, meeting the ocean tides;
And under the alders, that skirt its edge,
Now soft on the sand, now loud on the ledge,
Is heard the tramp of his steed as he rides.

It was twelve by the village clock
When he crossed the bridge into Medford town.
He heard the crowing of the cock,
And the barking of the farmer's dog,

And felt the damp of the river fog,
That rises after the sun goes down.

It was one by the village clock,
When he galloped into Lexington.
He saw the gilded weathercock
Swim in the moonlight as he passed,
And the meeting-house windows, blank and bare,
Gaze at him with a spectral glare,
As if they already stood aghast
At the bloody work they would look upon.

It was two by the village clock,
When he came to the bridge in Concord town.
He heard the bleating of the flock,
And the twitter of birds among the trees,
And felt the breath of the morning breeze
Blowing over the meadows brown.
And one was safe and asleep in his bed
Who at the bridge would be first to fall,
Who that day would be lying dead,
Pierced by a British musket-ball.

You know the rest. In the books you have read,
How the British Regulars fired and fled–
How the farmers gave them ball for ball,
From behind each fence and farmyard wall,
Chasing the red-coats down the lane,
Then crossing the fields to emerge again
Under the trees at the turn of the road,
And only pausing to fire and load.

So through the night rode Paul Revere;
And so through the night went his cry of alarm
To every Middlesex village and farm–
A cry of defiance and not of fear,
A voice in the darkness, a knock at the door,
And a word that shall echo forever-more!
For, borne on the night-wind of the Past,
Through all our history, to the last,
In the hour of darkness and peril and need,
The people will waken and listen to hear
The hurrying hoof-beats of that steed,
And the midnight message of Paul Revere.

Snow-White and Rose-Red

Traditional

Once upon a time there lived in a lonely cottage, surrounded by a garden, a poor widow. In the garden grew two rosebushes; one of them bore white roses, the other red.

Now the widow had two daughters, who so much resembled the rosebushes that she gave the name of Snow-white to one, and to the other Rose-red.

These two children were the best, the most obedient and most helpful children in the world. Snow-white was quiet and gentle; Rose-red was fond of running about the fields and meadows, in search of flowers and butterflies.

Snow-white would often stay at home with her mother, help her with the housework, and then read to her after it was done. The two children were very fond of each other, and when Snow-white would say, "We will never leave each other," her sister would reply, "No, never, as long as we live."

The mother added, "Whatever is given to one of you must be shared with the other."

They frequently rambled together alone in the wood to gather berries; and not a creature ever did them any harm, but all were quite friendly with them.

No danger ever threatened them, even if they stayed in the forest till nightfall. They would lie down on the mossy bed, and sleep safely till morning, and their mother knew there was no cause for fear.

Once, when they had remained in the wood all night, they did not awake till the rising sun had reddened the eastern sky, and as they opened their eyes they saw near them a beautiful little child, whose clothes were white and shining. When he saw they were awake, he looked kindly at them, and then, without a word, vanished from their sight.

When they glanced round, they found that they had been sleeping on the edge of a precipice, which they would have fallen into, had they moved in the dark. Their mother said it must have been one of the angels who watch over good children.

Snow-white and Rose-red kept their mother's cottage so neat and clean that it was a pleasure to look at it. Every morning in summer, Rose-red always took care to place by her mother's bed a bouquet of fresh flowers, in which was a bloom from each of the rosebushes. In winter Snow-white lit the fire, filled the kettle, and placed it over the blaze, where it shone and glittered like gold, for it was of burnished copper and was always kept bright.

In the evening, when the snow was falling, and the door closed and locked, they would seat themselves round the fire in the bright, snug little room, and knit busily, while their mother would put on her spectacles and read to them.

One evening there came a knock at the door, and the mother said, "Rose-red, open it quickly; no doubt some poor traveler, lost in the snow, wants shelter." Rose-red went and unbolted the door, when to her surprise, a great bear pushed his black head in.

Rose-red screamed aloud, and started back, and Snow-white hid herself behind her mother's bed.

The bear, however, began to speak very gently. "Do not fear," he said, "I will not hurt you. I only want to warm myself by your fire, for I am half frozen."

"Poor bear," said the mother, "come in and lie down by the fire, if you want to, but take care not to burn your furry coat."

Then she called out, "Snow-white and Rose-red, come here. The bear is quite gentle–he will do you no harm."

So they both came near to the fire, and gradually got over their fright.

The bear said, "Dear children, will you sweep off the snow from my fur?"

They fetched the broom and cleaned the bear's skin, till it looked quite smooth, and then he stretched himself at full length before the fire, grunting now and again, to show how contented and comfortable he felt. In a very short time they lost all fear of their unexpected guest.

When bedtime came, the mother said to him:

"You can stay here by the fire all night, if you like. I will not turn you out in this dreadful weather, and here you will at least be sheltered from the cold."

In the morning, when they all rose, the two children let the bear out, and he trotted away over the snow into the wood.

After that he came each evening at the same hour. They became so used to his visits that no one thought of bolting the door till the black fellow arrived. The winter passed, and spring was again covering the meadows and forest trees with her robe of green, and one morning the bear said to Snow-white: "I am going away now, during the summer, and you will not see me again till the end of autumn."

"Where are you going, dear bear?" asked Snow-white.

"I must go to the forest," he replied, "to hide my treasures from those wicked dwarfs. In winter these treasures are safe under the frozen earth, but now, when the sun has warmed and softened the ground, it is easy for them to break it and dig up what I have buried, and when once anything valuable is in their hands it is not easy to recover it."

Snow-white felt quite sorrowful when the bear said good-bye, but as he passed out of the door the latch caught his fur and tore a little piece off.

Snow-white thought she saw something glittering like gold under the skin, but she was not sure, for the bear trotted away very quickly and was soon lost from sight amongst the trees.

Some time after this the mother sent the children into the forest to gather brushwood, and they found a large tree that had fallen to the ground.

As they stood looking at it they saw something jumping up and down on the other side of the trunk, but they could not think what it was till they went nearer, and then they saw a little dwarf with a shriveled face, whose long white beard had been caught in the cleft of the tree. The dwarf was jumping about like a puppy at the end of a string, but he could not get free. He glared at the children with his red fiery eyes, and cried:

"Why do you stand there staring, instead of offering to assist me?"

"Poor little man," said Rose-red, "how did you do this?"

"You stupid goose!" he replied angrily. "I wanted to split up the tree so that I might get some shavings for our cooking. A great coal fire burns up our little dinners and suppers—we don't cram ourselves with food as you greedy people do. I drove my wedge into the tree and it seemed all right, but the horrid thing was so slippery that it sprang out again suddenly, and the tree closed so quickly that it caught my long white beard, and now holds it so fast that I cannot pull it out. See how the milk-faced creatures laugh!" he shouted. "Oh, but you are ugly!"

Despite his mean words and looks, the children wished to help him, and they went up to him and tried to pull out the beard—but all to no purpose.

"I will run home and call somebody," said Rose-red.

"What?" snarled the dwarf. "Send for more people! Why, there are two too many already, you sheep-headed madcaps!"

"Don't be impatient," said Snow-white. "I think we can manage to release you."

She took her scissors out of her pocket as she spoke, and cut the dwarf's beard off close to the trunk of the tree. No sooner was he at liberty than he caught hold of a bag full of gold that was lying among the roots, grumbling all the time about the dreadful children who had cut off his magnificent beard, a loss that nothing could make good. He then swung the bag across his shoulders, and went away without one word of thanks to the children for helping him.

Another day later on, Snow-white and Rose-red went out to catch fish. As they came near the banks of the stream they saw something like a large grasshopper jumping about, as if it were going to jump into the water. They ran forward, and recognized the dwarf.

"What are you doing here?" asked Rose-red. "Why do you wish to jump into the water?"

"Do you think I am such a fool as that?" he cried. "Don't you see how this dreadful fish is dragging me?"

The little man had been angling, but unfortunately the wind caught his beard and tangled it in the line, so that when a large fish came up and swallowed the bait he had not the strength to extricate himself, and the fish, in its efforts to escape, was dragging the dwarf into the water. He held tightly to the reeds and rushes that grew on the bank, but with very little effect, and the children were only just in time to save him from being dragged in by the fish.

They both pulled him back with all their might, but as long as the beard remained tangled in the line their efforts were useless, and they could not disentangle it. There remained no other means of saving him other than cutting off his beard, and this time so much of it that only a short piece remained.

When he saw this, the dwarf went into a dreadful rage. He screamed out, "Is it your custom, you wretches, to disfigure people's faces in this way? Not satisfied with cutting off a large piece the other day, you must now deprive me of nearly all. I dare not show myself such a fright as this. I wish you were made to run till you had lost the soles off your shoes!"

He lifted a bag of pearls that he had hidden among the rushes, and throwing it on his shoulder without another word, slunk away and disappeared behind a stone.

It happened on another occasion that the mother of the two girls sent them to the town to purchase needles, thread, and ribbon. Their way ran across a heath, on which here and there great rocks lay scattered.

Presently they saw a large bird hovering over a certain spot on the heath, till at last it pounced down suddenly to the earth, and at the same moment they heard terrible cries and piteous lamentations close to them. The children ran to the place, and saw with great alarm that a large eagle had their old acquaintance the dwarf in its talons, and was carrying him away. The good-natured children did all they could; they held the little man fast to pull him back, and struggled so fiercely that at last the eagle relinquished its prey and set him free.

But he had no sooner recovered from his fright than the ungrateful little wretch exclaimed: "What do you mean by catching hold of me so roughly? You clawed at my new coat till it is nearly torn off my back, awkward little clowns that you are!"

Then he took up his sack of precious stones, and slipped away among the rocks. The girls were accustomed to his ingratitude, and did not mind it. So they went on their way to the town, and made their purchases.

On their return, while crossing the heath, they came unexpectedly again upon the dwarf, who had emptied his sack of precious stones in a quiet corner. The evening sun shone brightly on the glittering jewels, which sparkled and flashed out such beautiful colors in the golden light that the children stood and gazed in silent admiration.

"What are you standing there gaping at?" asked the dwarf, his usually gray face quite red with rage. He was going on with his spiteful words when suddenly a terrible growl was heard, and a large black bear rushed out of the thicket.

The dwarf sprang up in a great fright, but he could not escape to a place of concealment, for the bear stood just in his way. Then he cried out piteously in his agony: "Dear Mr. Bear, do spare my life! I will give you all my treasures, and those jewels that you can see lying there, if you will only grant me my life. Such a weak little creature as I am would scarcely be a mouthful for you. See, there are two nice little tender bits–those two wicked maidens. They are as fat as young quails. Just eat them instead of me."

But the bear paid no attention to his complaints. Without a word he lifted up his left forepaw, and with one stroke laid the ugly, wicked little wretch dead on the ground.

The maidens, in a fright, were running away. But the bear called to them: "Snow-white, Rose-red, don't be afraid–wait, and I will go home with you."

They instantly recognized his voice, and stood still till he came up to them, but as he approached, what was their astonishment to see the bearskin suddenly fall off, and instead of a rough bear there stood before them a handsome young man, with beautiful, gold-embroidered clothes!

"I am a king's son," he said. "That wicked dwarf, after robbing me of all I possessed, changed me into a bear, and I have been obliged to wander about the woods, watching my treasures, but not able to catch the dwarf and kill him until today. His death has set me free, and he has met with a well-deserved fate."

Not many years after this Snow-white was married to the prince, and Rose-red to his brother. Their mother lived for many years in great happiness with her children. The two rosebushes were brought to the castle and planted in the garden near the windows of the two sisters; and every year they bore the same beautiful red and white roses.

Knock-Knock . . . Who's There?

Knock-knock.

Who's there?

It's Tom Thumb

Tom Thumb who?

It'th time thumbbody opened thith door!

Knock-knock.

Who's there?

Cockadoodle.

Cockadoodle who?

Not cockadoodle who, you silly chicken, cockadoodle-doo!

Knock-knock.

Who's there?

Orange.

Orange who?

Orange you glad it's Friday?

Knock-knock.

Who's there?

Aesop.

Aesop who?

Aesop I saw a puddy tat!

Knock-knock.

Who's there?

Lettuce.

Lettuce who?

Lettuce in! It's cold out here!

Knock-knock.

Who's there?

Alex.

Alex who?

Alex the questions round here!

Knock-knock.

Who's there?

Dwayne.

Dwayne who?

Dwayne the bathtub, I'm dwowning!

Knock-knock.

Who's there?

Old Lady.

Old Lady, who?

I didn't know you could yodel!

Knock-knock.

Who's there?

Aaron.

Aaron who?

Aaron the side of caution!

Knock-knock.

Who's there?

Beets.

Beets who?

Beets me, I forgot my name.

Knock-knock.

Who's there?

Déjà.

Déjà who?

Not déjà *who,* déjà *vu.*

Knock-knock.

Who's there?

Flea.

Flea who?

Flea blind mice.

Knock-knock.

Who's there?

Europe.

Europe who?

Europe to no good!

Knock-knock.

Who's there?

Lena.

Lena who?

Lena little closer and I'll tell you!

Knock-knock.

Who's there?

Althea.

Althea who?

Althea later, alligator!

A Nonsense Song

Stephen Vincent Benét

Rosemary, Rosemary, let down your hair!
The cow's in the hammock, the crow's in the chair!
I was making you songs out of sawdust and silk,
But they came in to call and they spilt them like milk.

The cat's in the coffee, the wind's in the east,
He screams like a peacock and whines like a priest
And the saw of his voice makes my blood turn to mice–
So let down your long hair and shut off his advice!

Pluck out the thin hairpins and let the waves stream,
Brown-gold as brook-waters that dance through a dream,
Gentle-curled as young cloudlings, sweet-fragrant as bay,
Till it takes all the fierceness of living away.

Oh, when you are with me, my heart is white steel.
But the bat's in the belfry, the mold's in the meal,
And I think I hear skeletons climbing the stair!
–Rosemary, Rosemary, let down your bright hair!

Mrs. Rachel Lynde Is Properly Horrified

From *Anne of Green Gables*

L.M. Montgomery

Anne had been a fortnight at Green Gables before Mrs. Lynde arrived to inspect her. Mrs. Rachel, to do her justice, was not to blame for this. A severe and unseasonable attack of grippe had confined that good lady to her house ever since the occasion of her last visit to Green Gables. Mrs. Rachel was not often sick and had a well-defined contempt for people who were; but grippe, she asserted, was like no other illness on earth and could only be interpreted as one of the special visitations of Providence. As soon as her doctor allowed her to put her foot out-of-doors she hurried up to Green Gables, bursting with curiosity to see Matthew and Marilla's orphan, concerning whom all sorts of stories and suppositions had gone abroad in Avonlea.

Anne had made good use of every waking moment of that fortnight. Already she was acquainted with every tree and shrub about the place. She had discovered that a lane opened out below the apple orchard and ran up through a belt of woodland; and she had explored it to its furthest end in all its delicious vagaries of brook and bridge, fir coppice and wild cherry arch, corners thick with fern, and branching byways of maple and mountain ash.

She had made friends with the spring down in the hollow–that wonderful deep, clear, icy-cold spring; it was set about with smooth red sandstones and rimmed in by great palm-like clumps of water fern; and beyond it was a log bridge over the brook.

That bridge led Anne's dancing feet up over a wooded hill beyond, where perpetual twilight reigned under the straight, thick-growing firs and spruces; the only flowers there were myriads of delicate "June bells," those shyest and sweetest of woodland blooms, and a few pale, aerial starflowers, like the spirits of last year's blossoms. Gossamers glimmered like threads of silver among the trees and the fir boughs and tassels seemed to utter friendly speech.

All these raptured voyages of exploration were made in the odd half hours which she was allowed for play, and Anne talked Matthew and Marilla half-deaf over her discoveries. Not that Matthew complained, to be sure; he listened to it all with a wordless smile of enjoyment on his face; Marilla permitted the "chatter" until she found herself becoming too interested in it, whereupon she always promptly quenched Anne by a curt command to hold her tongue.

Anne was out in the orchard when Mrs. Rachel came, wandering at her own sweet will through the lush, tremulous grasses splashed with ruddy evening sunshine; so that good lady had an excellent chance to talk her illness fully over, describing every ache and pulse beat with such evident enjoyment that Marilla thought even grippe must bring its compensations. When details were exhausted Mrs. Rachel introduced the real reason of her call.

"I've been hearing some surprising things about you and Matthew."

"I don't suppose you are any more surprised than I am myself," said Marilla. "I'm getting over my surprise now."

"It was too bad there was such a mistake," said Mrs. Rachel sympathetically. "Couldn't you have sent her back?"

"I suppose we could, but we decided not to. Matthew took a fancy to her. And I must say I like her myself–although I admit she has her faults. The house seems a different place already. She's a real bright little thing."

Marilla said more than she had intended to say when she began, for she read disapproval in Mrs. Rachel's expression.

"It's a great responsibility you've taken on yourself," said that lady gloomily, "especially when you've never had any experience with children. You don't know much about her or her real disposition, I suppose, and there's no guessing how a child like that will turn out. But I don't want to discourage you I'm sure, Marilla."

"I'm not feeling discouraged," was Marilla's dry response. "When I make up my mind to do a thing it stays made up. I suppose you'd like to see Anne. I'll call her in."

Anne came running in presently, her face sparkling with the delight of her orchard rovings; but, abashed at finding herself in the unexpected presence of a stranger, she halted confusedly inside the door. She certainly was an odd-looking little creature in the short tight wincey dress she had worn from the asylum, below which her thin legs seemed ungracefully long. Her freckles were more numerous and obtrusive than ever; the wind had ruffled her hatless hair into over-brilliant disorder; it had never looked redder than at that moment.

"Well, they didn't pick you for your looks, that's sure and certain," was Mrs. Rachel Lynde's emphatic comment. Mrs. Rachel was one of those delightful and popular people who pride themselves on speaking their mind without fear or favor. "She's terrible skinny and homely, Marilla. Come here, child, and let me have a look at you. Lawful heart, did any one ever see such freckles? And hair as red as carrots! Come here, child, I say."

Anne "came there," but not exactly as Mrs. Rachel expected. With one bound she crossed the kitchen floor and stood before Mrs. Rachel, her face scarlet with anger, her lips quivering, and her whole slender form trembling from head to foot.

"I hate you," she cried in a choked voice, stamping her foot on the floor. "I hate you–I hate you–I hate you–" a louder stamp with each assertion of hatred. "How dare you call me skinny and ugly? How dare you say I'm freckled and redheaded? You are a rude, impolite, unfeeling woman!"

"Anne!" exclaimed Marilla in consternation.

But Anne continued to face Mrs. Rachel undauntedly, head up, eyes blazing, hands clenched, passionate indignation exhaling from her like an atmosphere.

"How dare you say such things about me?" she repeated vehemently. "How would you like to have such things said about you? How would you like to be told that you are fat and clumsy and probably hadn't a spark of imagination in you? I don't care if I do hurt your feelings by saying so! I hope I hurt them. You have hurt mine worse than they were ever hurt before even by Mrs. Thomas' intoxicated husband. And I'll NEVER forgive you for it, never, never!"

Stamp! Stamp!

"Did anybody ever see such a temper!" exclaimed the horrified Mrs. Rachel.

"Anne, go to your room and stay there until I come up," said Marilla, recovering her powers of speech with difficulty.

Anne, bursting into tears, rushed to the hall door, slammed it until the tins on the porch wall outside rattled in sympathy, and fled through the hall and up the stairs like a whirlwind. A subdued slam above told that the door of the east gable had been shut with equal vehemence.

"Well, I don't envy you your job bringing *that* up, Marilla," said Mrs. Rachel with unspeakable solemnity.

Marilla opened her lips to say she knew not what of apology or deprecation. What she did say was a surprise to herself then and ever afterwards.

"You shouldn't have twitted her about her looks, Rachel."

"Marilla Cuthbert, you don't mean to say that you are upholding her in such a terrible display of temper as we've just seen?" demanded Mrs. Rachel indignantly.

"No," said Marilla slowly, "I'm not trying to excuse her. She's been very naughty and I'll have to give her a talking to about it. But we must make allowances for her. She's never been taught what is right. And you *were* too hard on her, Rachel."

Marilla could not help tacking on that last sentence, although she was again surprised at herself for doing it. Mrs. Rachel got up with an air of offended dignity.

"Well, I see that I'll have to be very careful what I say after this, Marilla, since the fine feelings of orphans, brought from goodness knows where, have to be considered before anything else. Oh, no, I'm not vexed–don't worry yourself. I'm too sorry for you to leave any room for anger in my mind. You'll have your own troubles with that child. But if you'll take my advice–which I suppose you won't do, although I've brought up ten children and buried two–you'll do that 'talking to' you mention with a fair-sized birch switch. I should think *that* would be the most effective language for that kind of a child. Her temper matches her hair I guess. Well, good evening, Marilla. I hope you'll come down to see me often as usual. But you can't expect me to visit here again in a hurry, if I'm liable to be flown at and insulted in such a fashion. It's something new in *my* experience."

Whereat Mrs. Rachel swept out and away–if a fat woman who always waddled *could* be said to sweep away–and Marilla with a very solemn face betook herself to the east gable.

On the way upstairs she pondered uneasily as to what she ought to do. She felt no little dismay over the scene that had just been enacted. How unfortunate that Anne should have displayed such temper before Mrs. Rachel Lynde, of all people! Then Marilla suddenly became aware of an uncomfortable and rebuking consciousness that she felt more humiliation over this than sorrow over the discovery of such a serious defect in Anne's disposition. And how was she to punish her? The amiable suggestion of the birch switch–to the efficiency of which all of Mrs. Rachel's own children could have borne smarting testimony–did not appeal to Marilla. She did not believe she could whip a child. No, some other method of punishment must be found to bring Anne to a proper realization of the enormity of her offense.

Marilla found Anne face downward on her bed, crying bitterly, quite oblivious of muddy boots on a clean counterpane.

"Anne," she said not ungently.

No answer.

"Anne," with greater severity, "get off that bed this minute and listen to what I have to say to you."

Anne squirmed off the bed and sat rigidly on a chair beside it, her face swollen and tear-stained and her eyes fixed stubbornly on the floor.

"This is a nice way for you to behave. Anne! Aren't you ashamed of yourself?"

"She hadn't any right to call me ugly and redheaded," retorted Anne, evasive and defiant.

"You hadn't any right to fly into such a fury and talk the way you did to her, Anne. I was ashamed of you–thoroughly ashamed of you. I wanted you to behave nicely to Mrs. Lynde, and instead of that you have disgraced me. I'm sure I don't know why you should lose your temper like that just because Mrs. Lynde said you were redhaired and homely. You say it yourself often enough."

"Oh, but there's such a difference between saying a thing yourself and hearing other people say it," wailed Anne. "You may know a thing is so, but you can't help hoping other people don't quite think it is. I suppose you think I have an awful temper, but I couldn't help it. When she said those things something just rose right up in me and choked me. I *had* to fly out at her."

"Well, you made a fine exhibition of yourself I must say. Mrs. Lynde will have a nice story to tell about you everywhere–and she'll tell it, too. It was a dreadful thing for you to lose your temper like that, Anne."

"Just imagine how you would feel if somebody told you to your face that you were skinny and ugly," pleaded Anne tearfully.

An old remembrance suddenly rose up before Marilla. She had been a very small child when she had heard one aunt say of her to another, "What a pity she is such a dark, homely little thing." Marilla was every day of fifty before the sting had gone out of that memory.

"I don't say that I think Mrs. Lynde was exactly right in saying what she did to you, Anne," she admitted in a softer tone. "Rachel is too outspoken. But that is no excuse for such behavior on your part. She was a stranger and an elderly person and my visitor–all three very good reasons why you should have been respectful to her. You were rude and saucy and"–Marilla had a saving inspiration of punishment–"you must go to her and tell her you are very sorry for your bad temper and ask her to forgive you."

"I can never do that," said Anne determinedly and darkly. "You can punish me in any way you like, Marilla. You can shut me up in a dark, damp dungeon inhabited by snakes and toads and feed me only on bread and water and I shall not complain. But I cannot ask Mrs. Lynde to forgive me."

"We're not in the habit of shutting people up in dark damp dungeons," said Marilla dryly, "especially as they're rather scarce in Avonlea. But apologize to Mrs. Lynde you must and shall, and you'll stay here in your room until you can tell me you're willing to do it."

"I shall have to stay here forever then," said Anne mournfully, "because I can't tell Mrs. Lynde I'm sorry I said those things to her. How can I? I'm *not* sorry. I'm sorry I've vexed you; but I'm *glad* I told her just what I did. It was a great satisfaction. I can't say I'm sorry when I'm not, can I? I can't even *imagine* I'm sorry."

"Perhaps your imagination will be in better working order by the morning," said Marilla, rising to depart. "You'll have the night to think over your conduct and come to a better frame of mind. You said you would try to be a very good girl if we kept you at Green Gables, but I must say it hasn't seemed very much like it this evening."

Leaving this Parthian shaft to rankle in Anne's stormy bosom, Marilla descended to the kitchen, grievously troubled in mind and vexed in soul. She was as angry with herself as with Anne, because, whenever she recalled Mrs. Rachel's dumbfounded countenance her lips twitched with amusement and she felt a most reprehensible desire to laugh.

Pooh's Rules of Etiquette When Entertaining

When unexpected guests show up in the evening, it is gracious to offer them a meal and a place to sleep. It is not necessary to give them your bed, however, especially if their visit got you up out of it.

If a guest should turn down your favorite food,
try to sound Sad and Regretful.

Near the end of a meal, it is polite to ask your guests if they would like a little more. But it is a good idea to check first to see if there is any more to give them.

When your guests prepare to leave, act sorry to see them go. But if it seems as though they may never leave, a subtle nudge is appropriate.

The Owl and the Pussy-Cat

Edward Lear

The Owl and the Pussy-Cat went to sea
In a beautiful pea-green boat,
They took some honey, and plenty of money,
Wrapped up in a five-pound note.

The Owl looked up to the stars above,
And sang to a small guitar,
"O lovely Pussy! O Pussy, my love,
What a beautiful Pussy you are, you are!
What a beautiful Pussy you are!"

Pussy said to the Owl, "You elegant fowl!
How charmingly sweet you sing!
O let us be married! Too long we have tarried.
But what shall we do for a ring?"

They sailed away for a year and a day,
To the land where the Bong tree grows,
And there in a wood a Piggy-wig stood,
With a ring at the end of his nose, his nose,
With a ring at the end of his nose.

"Dear Pig, are you willing to sell for one shilling
Your ring?" Said the Piggy, "I will."
So they took it away, and were married next day
By the Turkey who lives on the hill.

They dined on mince and slices of quince,
Which they ate with a runcible spoon;
And hand in hand, on the edge of the sand,
They danced by the light of the moon, the moon,
They danced by the light of the moon.

The Man of the Island

From *Treasure Island*

Robert Louis Stevenson

From the side of the hill, which was here steep and stony, a spout of gravel was dislodged, and fell rattling and bounding through the trees. My eyes turned instinctively in that direction, and I saw a figure leap with great rapidity behind the trunk of a pine. What it was, whether bear or man or monkey, I could in no wise tell. It seemed dark and shaggy; more I knew not. But the terror of this new apparition brought me to a stand.

I was now, it seemed, cut off upon both sides; behind me the murderers, before me this lurking nondescript. And immediately I began to prefer the dangers that I knew to those I knew not. Silver himself appeared less terrible in contrast with this creature of the woods, and I turned on my heel, and, looking sharply behind me over my shoulder, began to retrace my steps in the direction of the boats.

Instantly the figure reappeared, and, making a wide circuit, began to head me off. I was tired, at any rate; but had I been as fresh as when I rose, I could see it was in vain for me to contend in speed with such an adversary. From trunk to trunk the creature flitted like a deer, running man-like on two legs, but unlike any man that I had ever seen, stooping almost double as it ran. Yet a man it was, I could no longer be in doubt about that.

I began to recall what I had heard of cannibals. I was within an ace of calling for help. But the mere fact that he was a man, however wild, had somewhat reassured me, and my fear of Silver began to revive in proportion. I stood still therefore, and cast about for some method of escape; and as I was so thinking, the recollection of my pistol flashed into my mind. As soon as I remembered I was not defenseless, courage glowed again in my heart; and I set my face resolutely for this man of the island, and walked briskly towards him.

He was concealed, by this time, behind another tree trunk; but he must have been watching me closely, for as soon as I began to move in his direction he reappeared and took a step to meet me. Then he hesitated, drew back, came forward again, and at last, to my wonder and confusion, threw himself on his knees and held out his clasped hands in supplication.

At that I once more stopped.

"Who are you?" I asked.

"Ben Gunn," he answered, and his voice sounded hoarse and awkward, like a rusty lock. "I'm poor Ben Gunn, I am; and I haven't spoke with a Christian these three years."

I could now see that he was a white man like myself, and that his features were even pleasing. His skin, wherever it was exposed, was burnt by the sun; even his lips were black; and his fair eyes looked quite startling in so dark a face. Of all the beggar-men that I had seen or fancied, he was the chief for raggedness. He was clothed with tatters of old ships' canvas and old sea cloth; and this extraordinary patchwork was all held together by a system of the most various and incongruous fastenings, brass buttons, bits of stick, and loops of tarry gaskin. About his waist he wore an old brass-buckled leather belt, which was the one thing solid in his whole accoutrement.

"Three years!" I cried. "Were you shipwrecked?"

"Nay, mate," said he–"marooned."

I had heard the word, and I knew it stood for a horrible kind of punishment common enough among the buccaneers, in which the offender is put ashore with a little powder and shot and left behind on some desolate and distant island.

"Marooned three years agone," he continued, "and lived on goats since then, and berries, and oysters. Wherever a man is, says I, a man can do for himself. But, mate, my heart is sore for Christian diet. You mightn't happen to have a piece of cheese about you, now? No? Well, many's the long night I've dreamed of cheese–toasted, mostly–and woke up again, and here I were."

"If ever I can get aboard again," said I, "you shall have cheese by the stone."

All this time he had been feeling the stuff of my jacket, smoothing my hands, looking at my boots, and generally, in the intervals of his speech, showing a childish pleasure in the presence of a fellow creature. But at my last words he perked up into a kind of startled slyness.

"If ever you can get aboard again, says you?" he repeated. "Why, now, who's to hinder you?"

"Not you, I know," was my reply.

"And right you was," he cried. "Now you–what do you call yourself, mate?"

"Jim," I told him.

"Jim, Jim," says he, quite pleased apparently. "Well, now, Jim, I've lived that rough as you'd be ashamed to hear of. Now, for instance, you wouldn't think I had had a pious mother–to look at me?" he asked.

"Why, no, not in particular," I answered.

"Ah, well," said he, "but I had–remarkable pious. And I was a civil, pious boy, and could rattle off my catechism that fast, as you couldn't tell one word from another. And here's what it come to, Jim, and it begun with chuck-farthen on the blessed grave-stones! That's what it begun with, but it went further'n that; and so my mother told me, and predict'd the whole, she did, the pious woman! But it were Providence that put me here. I've thought it all out in this here lonely island, and I'm back on piety. You don't catch me tasting rum so much, but just a thimbleful for luck, of course, the first chance I have. I'm bound I'll be good, and I see the way to. And, Jim"–looking all round him and lowering his voice to a whisper–"I'm rich."

I now felt sure that the poor fellow had gone crazy in his solitude, and I suppose I must have shown the feeling in my face, for he repeated the statement hotly:

"Rich! Rich! I says. And I'll tell you what: I'll make a man of you, Jim. Ah, Jim, you'll bless your stars, you will, you was the first that found me!"

And at this there came suddenly a lowering shadow over his face, and he tightened his grasp upon my hand and raised a forefinger threateningly before my eyes.

"Now, Jim, you tell me true: that ain't Flint's ship?" he asked.

At this I had a happy inspiration. I began to believe that I had found an ally, and I answered him at once.

"It's not Flint's ship, and Flint is dead; but I'll tell you true, as you ask me–there are some of Flint's hands aboard; worse luck for the rest of us."

"Not a man–with one–leg?" he gasped.

"Silver?" I asked.

"Ah, Silver!" says he. "That were his name."

"He's the cook, and the ringleader too."

He was still holding me by the wrist, and at that he give it quite a wring.

"If you was sent by Long John," he said, "I'm as good as pork, and I know it. But where was you, do you suppose?"

I had made my mind up in a moment, and by way of answer told him the whole story of our voyage and the predicament in which we found ourselves. He heard me with the keenest interest, and when I had done he patted me on the head.

"You're a good lad, Jim," he said; "and you're all in a clove hitch, ain't you? Well, you just put your trust in Ben Gunn–Ben Gunn's the man to do it. Would you think it likely, now, that your squire would prove a liberal-minded one in case of help–him being in a clove hitch, as you remark?"

I told him the squire was the most liberal of men.

"Ay, but you see," returned Ben Gunn, "I didn't mean giving me a gate to keep, and a suit of livery clothes, and such; that's not my mark, Jim. What

I mean is, would he be likely to come down to the tune of, say one thousand pounds out of money that's as good as a man's own already?"

"I am sure he would," said I. "As it was, all hands were to share."

"*And* a passage home?" he added with a look of great shrewdness.

"Why," I cried, "the squire's a gentleman. And besides, if we got rid of the others, we should want you to help work the vessel home."

"Ah," said he, "so you would." And he seemed very much relieved.

"Now, I'll tell you what," he went on. "So much I'll tell you, and no more. I were in Flint's ship when he buried the treasure; he and six along–six strong seamen. They was ashore nigh on a week, and us standing off and on in the old *Walrus*. One fine day up went the signal, and here come Flint by himself in a little boat, and his head done up in a blue scarf. The sun was getting up, and mortal white he looked about the cutwater. But, there he was, you mind, and the six all dead–dead and buried. How he done it, not a man aboard us could make out. It was battle, murder, and sudden death, leastways–him against six. Billy Bones was the mate; Long John, he was quartermaster; and they asked him where the treasure was. 'Ah,' says he, 'you can go ashore, if you like, and stay,' he says; 'but as for the ship, she'll beat up for more, by thunder!' That's what he said.

"Well, I was in another ship three years back, and we sighted this island. 'Boys,' said I, 'here's Flint's treasure; let's land and find it.' The cap'n was displeased at that, but my messmates were all of a mind and landed. Twelve days they looked for it, and every day they had the worse word for me, until one fine morning all hands went aboard. 'As for you, Benjamin Gunn,' says they, 'here's a musket,' they says, 'and a spade, and pick-axe. You can stay here and find Flint's money for yourself,' they says.

"Well, Jim, three years have I been here, and not a bite of Christian diet from that day to this. But now, you look here; look at me. Do I look like a man before the mast? No, says you. Nor I weren't, neither, I says."

And with that he winked and pinched me hard.

"Just you mention them words to your squire, Jim," he went on. "Nor he weren't, neither–that's the words. Three years he were the man of this island, light and dark, fair and rain; and sometimes he would maybe think upon a prayer (says you), and sometimes he would maybe think of his old mother, so be as she's alive (you'll say); but the most part of Gunn's time (this is what you'll say)–the most part of his time was took up with another matter. And then you'll give him a nip, like I do."

And he pinched me again in the most confidential manner.

"Then," he continued, "then you'll up, and you'll say this: Gunn is a good man (you'll say), and he puts a precious sight more confidence–a precious sight, mind that–in a gen'leman born than in these gen'leman of fortune, having been one hisself."

"Well," I said, "I don't understand one word that you've been saying. But that's neither here nor there; for how am I to get on board?"

"Ah," said he, "that's the hitch, for sure. Well, there's my boat, that I made with my two hands. I keep her under the white rock. If the worst come to the worst, we might try that after dark. Hi!" he broke out. "What's that?"

For just then, although the sun had still an hour or two to run, all the echoes of the island awoke and bellowed to the thunder of a cannon.

"They have begun to fight!" I cried. "Follow me."

And I began to run towards the anchorage, my terrors all forgotten, while close at my side the marooned man in his goatskins trotted easily and lightly.

"Left, left," says he; "keep to your left hand, mate Jim! Under the trees with you! Theer's where I killed my first goat. They don't come down here now; they're all mastheaded on them mountings for the fear of Benjamin Gunn. Ah! And there's the cetemery"–cemetery, he must have meant. "You see the mounds? I come here and prayed, nows and thens, when I thought maybe a Sunday would be about due. It weren't quite a chapel, but it seemed more solemn like; and then, says you, Ben Gunn was short-handed–no chapling, nor so much as a Bible and a flag, you says."

So he kept talking as I ran, neither expecting nor receiving any answer.

The cannon-shot was followed after a considerable interval by a volley of small arms.

Another pause, and then, not a quarter of a mile in front of me, I beheld the Union Jack flutter in the air above a wood.

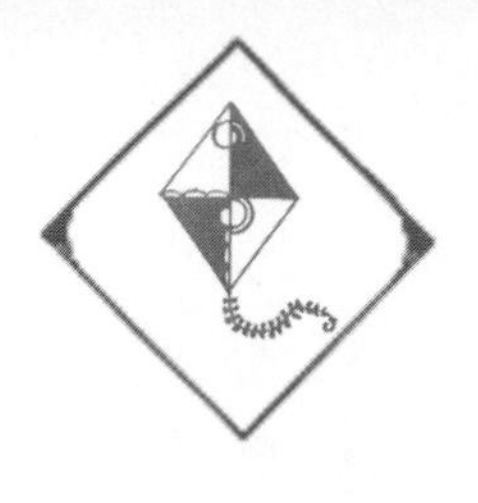

JABBERWOCKY

LEWIS CARROLL

Twas brillig, and the slithy toves
    Did gyre and gimble in the wabe;
All mimsy were the borogoves,
    And the mome raths outgrabe.

"Beware the Jabberwock, my son!
    The jaws that bite, the claws that catch!
Beware the Jubjub bird, and shun
    The frumious Bandersnatch!"

He took his vorpal sword in hand:
    Long time the manxome foe he sought–
So rested he by the Tumtum tree,
    And stood awhile in thought.

And as in uffish thought he stood,
    The Jabberwock, with eyes of flame,
Came whiffling through the tulgey wood,
    And burbled as it came!

One, two! One, two! And through and through
The vorpal blade went snicker-snack!
He left it dead, and with its head
He went galumphing back.

"And hast thou slain the Jabberwock?
Come to my arms, my beamish boy!
O frabjous day! Callooh! Callay!"
He chortled in his joy.

'Twas brillig, and the slithy toves
Did gyre and gimble in the wabe;
All mimsy were the borogoves,
And the mome raths outgrabe.

Wynken, Blynken, and Nod

Eugene Field

Wynken, Blynken, and Nod one night
Sailed off in a wooden shoe–
Sailed on a river of crystal light,
Into a sea of dew.
"Where are you going, and what do you wish?"
The old moon asked the three.
"We have come to fish for the herring-fish
That live in this beautiful sea;
Nets of silver and gold have we!"
Said Wynken, Blynken, and Nod.

The old moon laughed and sang a song,
As they rocked in the wooden shoe,
And the wind that sped them all night long,
Ruffled the waves of dew.
The little stars were the herring-fish
That lived in that beautiful sea–
"Now cast your nets wherever you wish–

But never afeard are we,"
So cried the stars to the fishermen three:
Wynken, Blynken, and Nod.

All night long their nets they threw
For the fish in the twinkling foam–
Then down from the sky came the wooden shoe,
Bringing the fishermen home;
'Twas all so pretty a sail, it seemed
As if it could not be;
And some folks thought 'twas a dream they'd dreamed
Of sailing that beautiful sea–
But I shall name you the fishermen three:
Wynken, Blynken, and Nod.

Wynken and Blynken are two little eyes,
And Nod is a little head,
And the wooden shoe that sailed the skies
Is a wee one's trundle bed.
So shut your eyes while mother sings
Of wonderful sights that be,
And you shall see the beautiful things
As you rock in the misty sea,
Where the old shoe rocked the fishermen three:
Wynken, Blynken, and Nod.

The Pirate Ship

From *Peter Pan & Wendy*

J.M. Barrie

One green light squinting over Kidd's Creek, which is near the mouth of the pirate river, marked where the brig, the *Jolly Roger,* lay, low in the water; a rakish-looking craft foul to the hull, every beam in her detestable like ground strewn with mangled feathers. She was the cannibal of the seas, and scarce needed that watchful eye, for she floated immune in the horror of her name.

She was wrapped in the blanket of night, through which no sound from her could have reached the shore. There was little sound, and none agreeable save the whir of the ship's sewing machine at which Smee sat, ever industrious and obliging, the essence of the commonplace, pathetic Smee. I know not why he was so infinitely pathetic, unless it were because he was so pathetically unaware of it; but even strong men had to turn hastily from looking at him, and more than once on summer evenings he had touched the fount of Hook's tears and made it flow. Of this, as of almost everything else, Smee was quite unconscious.

A few of the pirates leant over the bulwarks drinking in the miasma of the night; others sprawled by barrels over games of dice and cards; and the exhausted four who had carried the little house lay prone on the deck, where even in their sleep they rolled skillfully to this side or that out of Hook's reach, lest he should claw them mechanically in passing.

Hook trod the deck in thought. O man unfathomable. It was his hour of triumph. Peter had been removed forever from his path, and all the other boys were on the brig, about to walk the plank. It was his grimmest deed since the days when he had brought Barbecue to heel; and knowing as we do how vain a tabernacle is man, could we be surprised had he now paced the deck unsteadily, bellied out by the winds of his success?

But there was no elation in his gait, which kept pace with the action of his somber mind. Hook was profoundly dejected.

He was often thus when communing with himself on board ship in the quietude of the night. It was because he was so terribly alone. This inscrutable man never felt more alone than when surrounded by his dogs. They were socially so inferior to him.

Hook was not his true name. To reveal who he really was would even at this date set the country in a blaze; but as those who read between the lines must already have guessed, he had been at a famous public school; and its traditions still clung to him like garments, with which indeed they are largely concerned. Thus it was offensive to him even now to board a ship in the same dress in which he grappled her; and he still adhered in his walk to the school's distinguished slouch. But above all he retained the passion for good form.

Good form! However much he may have degenerated, he still knew that this is all that really matters.

From far within him he heard a creaking as of rusty portals, and through them came a stern tap-tap-tap, like hammering in the night when one cannot sleep. "Have you been good form today?" was their eternal question.

"Fame, fame, that glittering bauble, it is mine," he cried.

"Is it quite good form to be distinguished at anything?" the tap-tap from his school replied.

"I am the only man whom Barbecue feared," he urged; "and Flint himself feared Barbecue."

"Barbecue, Flint–what house?" came the cutting retort.

Most disquieting reflection of all, was it not bad form to think about good form?

His vitals were tortured by this problem. It was a claw within him sharper than the iron one; and as it tore him, the perspiration dripped down his sallow countenance and streaked his doublet. Several times he drew his sleeve across his face, but there was no damming that trickle.

Ah, envy not Hook.

There came to him a foreboding of his early dissolution. It was as if Peter's terrible oath had boarded the ship. Hook felt a gloomy desire to make his dying speech, lest presently there should be no time for it.

"Better for Hook," he cried, "if he had had less ambition." It was in his darkest hours only that he referred to himself in the third person.

"No little children love me."

Strange that he should think of this, which had never troubled him before; perhaps the sewing machine brought it to his mind. For long he muttered to himself, staring at Smee, who was hemming placidly, under the conviction that all children feared him.

Feared him! Feared Smee! There was not a child on board the brig that night who did not already love him. He had said horrid things to them and hit them with the palm of his hand, because he could not hit with his fist; but they had only clung to him the more. Michael had tried on his spectacles.

To tell poor Smee that they thought him lovable! Hook itched to do it, but it seemed too brutal. Instead, he revolved this mystery in his mind: why do they find Smee lovable? He pursued the problem like the sleuth hound that he was. If Smee was lovable, what was it that made him so? A terrible answer suddenly presented itself: "Good form?"

Had the bo'sun good form without knowing it, which is the best form of all?

He remembered that you have to prove you don't know you have it before you arc eligible for Pop.

With a cry of rage he raised his iron hand over Smee's head; but he did not tear. What arrested him was this reflection:

"To claw a man because he is good form, what would that be?"

"Bad form!"

The unhappy Hook was as impotent as he was damp, and he fell forward like a cut flower.

His dogs thinking him out of the way for a time, discipline instantly relaxed; and they broke into a bacchanalian dance, which brought him to his feet at once; all traces of human weakness gone, as if a bucket of water had passed over him.

"Quiet, you scugs," he cried, "or I'll cast anchor in you," and at once the din was hushed. "Are all the children chained, so they cannot fly away?"

"Ay, ay."

"Then hoist them up."

The wretched prisoners were dragged from the hold, all except Wendy, and ranged in line in front of him. For a time he seemed unconscious of their presence. He lolled at his ease, humming, not unmelodiously, snatches of a rude song, and fingering a pack of cards. Ever and anon the light from his cigar gave a touch of color to his face.

"Now then, bullies," he said briskly, "six of you walk the plank tonight, but I have room for two cabin boys. Which of you is it to be?"

"Don't irritate him unnecessarily," had been Wendy's instructions in the hold; so Tootles stepped forward politely. Tootles hated the idea of signing under such a man, but an instinct told him that it would be prudent to lay the responsibility on an absent person; and though a somewhat silly boy, he knew that mothers alone are always willing to be the buffer. All children know this about mothers, and despise them for it, but make constant use of it.

So Tootles explained prudently, "You see, sir, I don't think my mother would like me to be a pirate. Would your mother like you to be a pirate, Slightly?"

He winked at Slightly, who said mournfully, "I don't think so," as if he wished things had been otherwise. "Would your mother like you to be a pirate, Twin?"

"I don't think so," said the first twin, as clever as the others. "Nibs, would–"

"Stow this gab," roared Hook, and the spokesmen were dragged back. "You, boy," he said, addressing John, "you look as if you had a little pluck in you. Didst never want to be a pirate, my hearty?"

Now John had sometimes experienced this hankering at maths prep., and he was struck by Hook's picking him out.

"I once thought of calling myself Red-handed Jack," he said diffidently.

"And a good name too. We'll call you that here, bully, if you join."

"What do you think, Michael?" asked John.

"What would you call me if I join?" Michael demanded.

"Blackbeard Joe."

Michael was naturally impressed. "What do you think, John?" He wanted John to decide, and John wanted him to decide.

"Shall we still be respectful subjects of the King?" John inquired.

Through Hook's teeth came the answer: "You would have to swear, 'Down with the King.'"

Perhaps John had not behaved very well so far, but he shone out now.

"Then I refuse," he cried, banging the barrel in front of Hook.

"And I refuse," cried Michael.

"Rule Britannia!" squeaked Curly.

The infuriated pirates buffeted them in the mouth; and Hook roared out, "That seals your doom. Bring up their mother. Get the plank ready."

They were only boys, and they went white as they saw Jukes and Cecco preparing the fatal plank. But they tried to look brave when Wendy was brought up.

No words of mine can tell you how Wendy despised those pirates. To the boys there was at least some glamour in the pirate calling, but all that she saw was that the ship had not been scrubbed for years. There was not a porthole on the grimy glass of which you might not have written with your finger "Dirty pig," and she had already written it on several. But as the boys gathered round her she had no thought, of course, save for them.

"So, my beauty," said Hook, as if he spoke in syrup, "you are to see your children walk the plank."

Fine gentleman though he was, the intensity of his communings had soiled his ruff, and suddenly he knew that she was gazing at it. With a hasty gesture he tried to hide it, but he was too late.

"Are they to die?" asked Wendy, with a look of such frightful contempt that he nearly fainted.

"They are," he snarled. "Silence all," he called gloatingly, "for a mother's last words to her children."

At this moment Wendy was grand. "These are my last words, dear boys," she said firmly. "I feel that I have a message to you from your real mothers, and it is this: 'We hope our sons will die like English gentlemen.'"

Even the pirates were awed; and Tootles cried out hysterically, "I am going to do what my mother hopes. What are you to do, Nibs?"

"What my mother hopes. What are you to do, Twin?"

"What my mother hopes. John, what are–"

But Hook had found his voice again.

"Tie her up," he shouted.

It was Smee who tied her to the mast. "See here, honey," he whispered, "I'll save you if you promise to be my mother."

But not even for Smee would she make such a promise. "I would almost rather have no children at all," she said disdainfully.

It is sad to know that not a boy was looking at her as Smee tied her to the mast; the eyes of all were on the plank: that last little walk they were about to take. They were no longer able to hope that they would walk it manfully, for the capacity to think had gone from them; they could stare and shiver only.

Hook smiled on them with his teeth closed, and took a step toward Wendy. His intention was to turn her face so that she should see the boys walking the plank one by one. But he never reached her, he never heard the cry of anguish he hoped to wring from her. He heard something else instead.

It was the terrible tick-tick of the crocodile.

They all heard it–pirates, boys, Wendy; and immediately every head was blown in one direction; not to the water whence the sound proceeded, but toward Hook. All knew that what was about to happen concerned him alone, and that from being actors they were suddenly become spectators.

Very frightful was it to see the change that came over him. It was as if he had been clipped at every joint. He fell in a little heap.

The sound came steadily nearer; and in advance of it came this ghastly thought, "The crocodile is about to board the ship."

Even the iron claw hung inactive; as if knowing that it was no intrinsic part of what the attacking force wanted. Left so fearfully alone, any other man would have lain with his eyes shut where he fell: but the gigantic brain of Hook was still working, and under its guidance he crawled on his knees along the deck as far from the sound as he could go. The pirates respectfully cleared a passage for him, and it was only when he brought up against the bulwarks that he spoke.

"Hide me," he cried hoarsely.

They gathered round him; all eyes averted from the thing that was coming aboard. They had no thought of fighting it. It was Fate.

Only when Hook was hidden from them did curiosity loosen the limbs of the boys so that they could rush to the ship's side to see the crocodile climbing it. Then they got the strangest surprise of this Night of Nights–for it was no crocodile that was coming to their aid. It was Peter.

He signed to them not to give vent to any cry of admiration that might rouse suspicion. Then he went on ticking.

The Ugly Duckling

Hans Christian Andersen

It was so glorious out in the country; it was summer; the cornfields were yellow, the oats were green, the hay had been put up in stacks in the green meadows, and the stork went about on his long red legs, and chattered Egyptian, for this was the language he had learned from his good mother. All around the fields and meadows were great forests, and in the midst of these forests lay deep lakes. Yes, it was right glorious out in the country. In the midst of the sunshine there lay an old farm, with deep canals about it, and from the wall down to the water grew great burdocks, so high that little children could stand upright under the loftiest of them. It was just as wild there as in the deepest wood, and here sat a Duck upon her nest; she had to hatch her ducklings; but she was almost tired out before the little ones came; and then she so seldom had visitors. The other ducks liked better to swim about in the canals than to run up to sit down under a burdock, and cackle with her.

At last one egg-shell after another burst open. "Piep! Piep!" it cried, and in all the eggs there were little creatures that stuck out their heads.

"Quack! quack!" they said; and they all came quacking out as fast as they could, looking all around them under the green leaves; and the mother let them look as much as they chose, for green is good for the eye.

"How wide the world is!" said all the young ones, for they certainly had much more room now than when they were in the eggs.

"D'ye think this is all the world?" said the mother. "That stretches far across the other side of the garden, quite into the parson's field; but I have never been there yet. I hope you are all together," and she stood up. "No, I have not all. The largest egg still lies there. How long is that to last? I am really tired of it." And she sat down again.

"Well, how goes it?" asked an old Duck who had come to pay her a visit.

"It lasts a long time with that one egg," said the Duck who sat there. "It will not burst. Now, only look at the others; are they not the prettiest little ducks one could possibly see? They are all like their father–the rogue, he never comes to see me."

"Let me see the egg which will not burst," said the old visitor. "You may be sure it is a turkey's egg. I was once cheated in that way, and had much anxiety and trouble with the young ones, for they are afraid of the water. I must tell you, I could not get them to venture in. I quacked and I clacked, but it was no use. Let me see the egg. Yes, that's a turkey's egg. Let it lie there, and teach the other children to swim."

"I think I will sit on it a little longer," said the Duck. "I've sat so long now that I can sit a few days more."

"Just as you please," said the old Duck; and she went away.

At last the great egg burst. "Peep! peep!" said the little one, and crept forth. It was very large and very ugly. The Duck looked at it.

"It's a very large duckling," said she; "none of the others look like that—can it really be a turkey chick? Well, we shall soon find out. It must go into the water, even if I have to thrust it in myself."

The next day, it was bright, beautiful weather; the sun shone on all the green trees. The Mother-Duck went down to the canal with all her family. Splash! She jumped into the water. "Quack! quack!" she said, and one duckling after another plunged in. The water closed over their heads, but they came up in an instant, and swam capitally; their legs went of themselves, and they were all in the water. The ugly gray Duckling swam with them.

"No, it's not a turkey," said she; "look how well it can use its legs, and how straight it holds itself. It is my own child! On the whole it's quite pretty, if one looks at it rightly. Quack! quack! come with me, and I'll lead you out into the great world, and present you in the duck-yard; but keep close to me, so that no one may tread on you, and take care of the cats!"

And so they came into the duck-yard. There was a terrible riot going on in there, for two families were quarreling about an eel's head, and the cat got it after all.

"See, that's how it goes in the world!" said the Mother-Duck; and she whetted her beak, for she too wanted the eel's head. "Only use your legs," she said. "See that you can bustle about, and bow your heads before the old Duck yonder. She's the grandest of all here; she's of Spanish blood—that's why she's so fat; and d'ye see? She has a red rag round her leg—that's something particularly fine, and the greatest distinction a duck can enjoy—it signifies that one does not want to lose her, and that she's to be known by the animals and by men too. Shake yourselves—don't turn in your toes; a well-brought-up duck turns its toes quite out, just like father and mother–so! Now bend your necks and say 'Quack!'"

And they did so: but the other ducks round about looked at them, and said quite boldly–

"Look there! Now we're to have these hanging on, as if there were not enough of us already! And–fie!–how that Duckling yonder looks; we won't stand that!" And one duck flew up at it, and bit it in the neck.

"Let him alone," said the mother; "he does no harm to any one."

"Yes, but he is too large and peculiar," said the Duck who had bitten him; "and therefore he must be put down."

"Those are pretty children that the mother has there," said the old Duck with the rag round her leg. "They're all pretty but that one; that was rather unlucky. I wish she could bear it over again."

"That cannot be done, my lady," replied the Mother-Duck. "He is not pretty, but he has a really good disposition, and swims as well as any other; yes, I may even say it, swims better. I think he will grow up pretty, and become smaller in time; he has lain too long in the egg, and therefore is not properly shaped." And then she pinched him in the neck, and smoothed his feathers. "Moreover he is a drake," she said, "and therefore it is not of so much consequence. I think he will be very strong–he makes his way already."

"The other ducklings are graceful enough," said the old Duck. "Make yourself at home; and if you find an eel's head, you may bring it to me."

And now they were at home. But the poor Duckling which had crept last out of the egg, and looked so ugly, was bitten and pushed and jeered, as much by the ducks as by the chickens.

"It is too big!" they all said. And the turkey-cock, who had been born with the spurs, and therefore thought himself an emperor, blew himself up like a ship in full sail, and bore straight down upon him; then he gobbled and grew quite red in the face. The poor Duckling did not know where he should stand or walk; he was quite melancholy because he looked ugly, and was the butt of the whole duck-yard.

So it went on the first day; and afterwards it became worse and worse. The poor Duckling was hunted about by every one; even his brothers and sisters were quite angry with him, and said, "If the cat would only catch you, you ugly creature!" And the mother said, "If you were only far away!" And the ducks bit him, and the chickens beat him, and the girl who had to feed the poultry kicked at him with her foot.

Then he ran and flew over the fence, and the little birds in the bushes flew up in fear.

"That is because I am so ugly!" thought the Duckling; and he shut his eyes, but flew on further; and so he came out into the great moor, where the wild ducks lived. Here he lay the whole night long and was weary and downcast.

Towards morning the wild ducks flew up, and looked at their new companion.

"What sort of a one are you?" they asked; and the Duckling turned in every direction, and bowed as well as he could. "You are remarkably ugly!"

said the Wild Ducks. "But that is nothing to us, so long as you do not marry into our family."

Poor thing! He certainly did not think of marrying, and only hoped to obtain leave to lie among the reeds and drink some of the swamp water.

Thus he lay two whole days; then came thither two wild geese, or, properly speaking, two wild ganders. It was not long since each had crept out of an egg, and that's why they were so saucy.

"Listen, comrade," said one of them. "You're so ugly that I like you. Will you go with us, and become a bird of passage? Near here, in another moor, there are a few sweet lovely wild geese, all unmarried, and all able to say 'Rap?' You've a chance of making your fortune, ugly as you are."

"Piff! Paff!" resounded through the air; and the two ganders fell down dead in the swamp, and the water became blood red. "Piff! Paff!" is sounded again, and the whole flock of wild geese rose up from the reeds. And then there was another report. A great hunt was going on. The sportsmen were lying in wait all round the moor, and some were even sitting up in the branches of the trees, which spread far over the reeds. The blue smoke rose up like clouds among the dark trees, and was wafted far away across the water; and the hunting dogs came–splash, splash!–into the swamp, and the rushes and the reeds bent down on every side. That was a fright for the poor Duckling! He turned his head, and put it under his wing; but at that moment a frightful great dog stood close by the Duckling. His tongue hung far out of his mouth, and his eyes gleamed horrible and ugly; he thrust out his nose close against the Duckling, showed his sharp teeth, and–splash, splash!–on he went, without seizing him.

"O, Heaven be thanked!" sighed the Duckling. "I am so ugly, that even the dog does not like to bite me!"

And so it lay quite quiet, while the shots rattled through the reeds and gun after gun was fired. At last, late in the day, all was still; but the poor Duckling did not dare to rise up; he waited several hours before he looked round, and then hastened away out of the moor as fast as he could. He ran on over field and meadow; there was such a storm raging that it was difficult to get from one place to another.

Towards evening the Duck came to a little miserable peasant's hut. This hut was so dilapidated that it did not itself know on which side it should fall; and that's why it remained standing. The storm whistled round the Duckling in such a way that the poor creature was obliged to sit down, to stand against it; and the wind blew worse and worse. Then the Duckling noticed that one of the hinges of the door had given way, and the door hung so slanting that the Duckling could slip through the crack into the room; and that is what he did.

Here lived a woman, with her Cat and her Hen. And the Cat, whom she called Sonnie, could arch his back and purr, he could even give out sparks; but for that one had to stroke his fur the wrong way. The Hen had quite little short legs, and therefore she was called Chickabiddy Shortshanks; she laid good eggs, and the woman loved her as her own child.

In the morning the strange Duckling was at once noticed, and the Cat began to purr and the Hen to cluck.

"What's this?" said the woman, and looked all round; but she could not see well, and therefore she thought the Duckling was a fat duck that had strayed. "This is a rare prize!" she said. "Now I shall have duck's eggs. I hope it is not a drake. We must try that."

And so the Duckling was admitted on trial for three weeks; but no eggs came. And the Cat was master of the house, and the Hen was the lady, and always said "We and the world!" for she thought they were half the world, and by far the better half. The Duckling thought one might have a different opinion, but the Hen would not allow it.

"Can you lay eggs?" she asked,

"No."

"Then will you hold your tongue!"

And the Cat said, "Can you curve your back, and purr, and give out sparks?"

"No."

"Then you will please have no opinion of your own when sensible folks are speaking."

And the Duckling sat in a corner and was melancholy; then the fresh air and the sunshine streamed in; and he was seized with such a strange longing to swim on the water, that he could not help telling the Hen of it.

"What are you thinking of?" cried the Hen. "You have nothing to do, that's why you have these fancies. Lay eggs, or purr, and they will pass over."

"But it is so charming to swim on the water!" said the Duckling, "so refreshing to let it close above one's head, and to dive down to the bottom."

"Yes, that must be a mighty pleasure, truly," said the Hen. "I fancy you must have gone crazy. Ask the Cat about it–he's the cleverest animal I know–ask him if he likes to swim on the water, or to dive down. I won't speak about myself. Ask our mistress, the old woman; no one in the world is clev-erer than she. Do you think she has any desire to swim, and to let the water close above her head?"

"You don't understand me," said the Duckling.

"We don't understand you? Then pray who is to understand you? You surely don't pretend to be cleverer than the Cat and the woman–I won't say anything of myself. Don't be conceited, child, and thank your Maker for all the kindness you have received. Did you not get into a warm room, and have you not fallen into company from which you may learn something? But you are a chatterer, and it is not pleasant to associate with you. You may believe me, I speak for your good. I tell you disagreeable things, and by that one may always know one's true friends! Only take care that you learn to lay eggs, or to purr, and give out sparks!"

"I think I will go out into the wide world," said the Duckling.

"Yes, do go," replied the Hen.

And so the Duckling went away. He swam on the water, and dived, but he was slighted by every creature because of his ugliness.

Now came the autumn. The leaves in the forest turned yellow and brown; the wind caught them so that they danced about, and up in the air it was very cold. The clouds hung low, heavy with hail and snowflakes, and on the fence stood the raven, crying, "Croak! croak!" for mere cold; yes, it was enough to make one feel cold to think of this. The poor little Duckling cer-tainly had not a good time. One evening–the sun was just setting in his beauty–there came a whole flock of great, handsome birds out of the bushes; they were dazzlingly white, with long, flexible necks; they were swans. They uttered a very peculiar cry, spread forth their glorious great wings, and flew away from that cold region to warmer lands, to fair open lakes. They mounted so high, so high! and the ugly Duckling felt quite strangely as it watched them. He turned round and round in the water like a wheel, stretched out his neck towards them, and uttered such a strange, loud cry as frightened himself. Oh! He could not forget those beautiful, happy birds; and so soon as he could see them no longer, he dived down to the very bottom, and when he came up again, he was quite beside himself. He knew not the name of those birds, and knew not whither they were flying; but he loved them more than he had ever loved any one. He was not at all envious of them. How could he think of wishing to possess such loveliness as they had? The Duckling would have been glad if only the ducks would have endured his company–the poor, ugly creature!

And the winter grew cold, very cold! The Duckling was forced to swim about in the water, to prevent the surface from freezing entirely; but every night the hole in which he swam about became smaller and smaller. It froze so hard that the icy covering crackled again; and the Duckling was obliged to use his legs continually to prevent the hole from freezing up. At last he became exhausted, and lay quite still, and thus froze fast into the ice.

Early in the morning a peasant came by, and when he saw what had happened, he took his wooden shoe, broke the ice-crust to pieces, and carried the Duckling home to his wife. Then the Duckling came to himself again. The children wanted to play with him; but the Duckling thought they wanted to hurt him, and in terror fluttered up into the milk-pan, so that the milk spurted down into the room. The woman clasped her hands, at which the

Duckling flew down into the butter-tub, and then into the meal barrel and out again. How he looked then! The woman screamed, and struck at him with the fire-tongs; the children tumbled over one another in their efforts to catch the Duckling; and they laughed and they screamed!—well it was that the door stood open, and the poor creature was able to slip out between the shrubs into the newly-fallen snow—there he lay quite exhausted.

But it would be too melancholy if I were to tell all the misery and care which the Duckling had to endure in the hard winter. He lay out on the moor among the reeds, when the sun began to shine again and the larks to sing—it was a beautiful spring.

Then all at once the Duckling could flap his wings—they beat the air more strongly than before, and bore it strongly away; and before it well knew how all this happened, he found himself in a great garden, where the elder trees smelled sweet, and bent their long green branches down to the canal that wound through the region. Oh, here it was so beautiful, such a gladness of spring! and from the thicket came three glorious white swans; they rustled their wings, and swam lightly on the water. The Duckling knew the splendid creatures, and felt oppressed by a peculiar sadness.

"I will fly away to them, to the royal birds; and they will beat me, because I, that am so ugly, dare to come near them. But it is all the same. Better be killed by *them* than to be pursued by ducks, and beaten by fowls, and pushed about by the girl who takes care of the poultry yard, and to suffer hunger in winter!" And he flew out into the water, and swam towards the beautiful swans. These looked at the Duckling, and came sailing down upon him with outspread wings. "Kill me!" said the poor creature, and bent his head down upon the water, expecting nothing but death. But what was this that he saw in the clear water? He beheld his own image; and it was no longer that of a clumsy dark-gray bird, ugly and hateful to look at, but a–swan!

It matters nothing if one is born in a duck-yard, if one has only lain in a swan's egg.

He felt quite glad at all the need and misfortune he had suffered; now he realized his happiness in all the splendor that surrounded him. And the great swans swam round, and stroked him with their beaks.

Into the garden came little children, who threw bread and corn into the water; and the youngest cried, "There is a new one!" and the other children shouted joyously, "Yes, a new one has arrived!" And they clapped their hands and danced about, and ran to their father and mother; and bread and cake were thrown into the water; and they all said, "The new one is the most beautiful of all! So young and handsome!" and the old swans bowed their heads before him.

Then he felt quite ashamed, and hid his head under his wings, for he did not know what to do; he was so happy, and yet not at all proud. He thought how he had been persecuted and despised; and now he heard them saying that he was the most beautiful of all birds. Even the elder tree bent its branches straight down into the water before him, and the sun shone warm and mild. Then his wings rustled, he lifted his slender neck, and cried rejoicingly from the depths of his heart–

"I never dreamed of so much happiness when I was the Ugly Duckling!"

THE COWARDLY LION

FROM *THE WONDERFUL WIZARD OF OZ*

L. FRANK BAUM

All this time Dorothy and her companions had been walking through the thick woods. The road was still paved with yellow brick, but these were much covered by dried branches and dead leaves from the trees, and the walking was not at all good.

There were few birds in this part of the forest, for birds love the open country where there is plenty of sunshine; but now and then there came a deep growl from some wild animal hidden among the trees. These sounds made the little girl's heart beat fast, for she did not know what made them; but Toto knew, and he walked close to Dorothy's side, and did not even bark in return.

"How long will it be," the child asked of the Tin Woodman, "before we are out of the forest?"

"I cannot tell," was the answer, "for I have never been to the Emerald City. But my father went there once, when I was a boy, and he said it was a long journey through a dangerous country, although nearer to the city where Oz dwells the country is beautiful. But I am not afraid so long as I have my oil-can, and nothing can hurt the Scarecrow, while you bear upon your forehead the mark of the good Witch's kiss, and that will protect you from harm."

"But Toto!" said the girl, anxiously; "what will protect him?"

"We must protect him ourselves, if he is in danger," replied the Tin Woodman.

Just as he spoke there came from the forest a terrible roar, and the next moment a great Lion bounded into the road. With one blow of his paw he sent the Scarecrow spinning over and over to the edge of the road, and then he struck at the Tin Woodman with his sharp claws. But, to the Lion's surprise, he could make no impression on the tin, although the Woodman fell over in the road and lay still.

Little Toto, now that he had an enemy to face, ran barking toward the Lion, and the great beast had opened his mouth to bite the dog, when Dorothy, fearing Toto would be killed, and heedless of danger, rushed forward and slapped the Lion upon his nose as hard as she could, while she cried out:

"Don't you dare to bite Toto! You ought to be ashamed of yourself, a big beast like you, to bite a poor little dog!"

"I didn't bite him," said the Lion, as he rubbed his nose with his paw where Dorothy had hit it.

"No, but you tried to," she retorted. "You are nothing but a big coward."

"I know it," said the Lion, hanging his head in shame; "I've always known it. But how can I help it?"

"I don't know, I'm sure. To think of your striking a stuffed man, like the poor Scarecrow!"

"Is he stuffed?" asked the Lion, in surprise, as he watched her pick up the Scarecrow and set him upon his feet, while she patted him into shape again.

"Of course he's stuffed," replied Dorothy, who was still angry.

"That's why he went over so easily," remarked the Lion. "It astonished me to see him whirl around so. Is the other one stuffed, also?"

"No," said Dorothy, "he's made of tin." And she helped the Woodman up again.

"That's why he nearly blunted my claws," said the Lion. "When they scratched against the tin it made a cold shiver run down my back. What is that little animal you are so tender of?"

"He is my dog, Toto," answered Dorothy.

"Is he made of tin, or stuffed?" asked the Lion.

"Neither. He's a–a–a meat dog," said the girl.

"Oh! He's a curious animal, and seems remarkably small, now that I look at him. No one would think of biting such a little thing except a coward like me," continued the Lion, sadly.

"What makes you a coward?" asked Dorothy, looking at the great beast in wonder, for he was as big as a small horse.

"It's a mystery," replied the Lion. "I suppose I was born that way. All the other animals in the forest naturally expect me to be brave, for the Lion is everywhere thought to be the King of Beasts. I learned that if I roared very loudly every living thing was frightened and got out of my way. Whenever I've met a man I've been awfully scared; but I just roared at him, and he has always run away as fast as he could go. If the elephants and the tigers and the bears had ever tried to fight me, I should have run myself–I'm such a coward; but just as soon as they hear me roar they all try to get away from me, and of course I let them go."

"But that isn't right. The King of Beasts shouldn't be a coward," said the Scarecrow.

"I know it," returned the Lion, wiping a tear from his eye with the tip of his tail; "it is my great sorrow, and makes my life very unhappy. But whenever there is danger my heart begins to beat fast."

"Perhaps you have heart disease," said the Tin Woodman.

"It may be," said the Lion.

"If you have," continued the Tin Woodman, "you ought to be glad, for it proves you have a heart. For my part, I have no heart; so I cannot have heart disease."

"Perhaps," said the Lion, thoughtfully, "if I had no heart I should not be a coward."

"Have you brains?" asked the Scarecrow.

"I suppose so. I've never looked to see," replied the Lion.

"I am going to the great Oz to ask him to give me some," remarked the Scarecrow, "for my head is stuffed with straw."

"And I am going to ask him to give me a heart," said the Woodman.

"And I am going to ask him to send Toto and me back to Kansas," added Dorothy.

"Do you think Oz could give me courage?" asked the cowardly Lion.

"Just as easily as he could give me brains," said the Scarecrow.

"Or give me a heart," said the Tin Woodman.

"Or send me back to Kansas," said Dorothy.

"Then, if you don't mind, I'll go with you," said the Lion, "for my life is simply unbearable without a bit of courage."

"You will be very welcome," answered Dorothy, "for you will help to keep away the other wild beasts. It seems to me they must be more cowardly than you are if they allow you to scare them so easily."

"They really are," said the Lion; "but that doesn't make me any braver, and as long as I know myself to be a coward I shall be unhappy."

So once more the little company set off upon the journey, the Lion walking with stately strides at Dorothy's side. Toto did not approve this new comrade at first, for he could not forget how nearly he had been crushed between the Lion's great jaws; but after a time he became more at ease, and presently Toto and the Cowardly Lion had grown to be good friends.

During the rest of that day there was no other adventure to mar the peace of their journey. Once, indeed, the Tin Woodman stepped upon a beetle that was crawling along the road, and killed the poor little thing. This made the Tin Woodman very unhappy, for he was always careful not to hurt any living creature; and as he walked along he wept several tears of sorrow and regret. These tears ran slowly down his face and over the hinges of his jaw, and there they rusted. When Dorothy presently asked him a question the Tin Woodman could not open his mouth, for his jaws were tightly rusted together. He became greatly frightened at this and made many motions to Dorothy to relieve him, but she could not understand. The Lion was also puzzled to know what was wrong. But the Scarecrow seized the oil-can from Dorothy's basket and oiled the Woodman's jaws, so that after a few moments he could talk as well as before.

"This will serve me a lesson," said he, "to look where I step. For if I should kill another bug or beetle I should surely cry again, and crying rusts my jaws so that I cannot speak."

Thereafter he walked very carefully, with his eyes on the road, and when he saw a tiny ant toiling by he would step over it, so as not to harm it. The Tin Woodman knew very well he had no heart, and therefore he took great care never to be cruel or unkind to anything.

"You people with hearts," he said, "have something to guide you, and need never do wrong; but I have no heart, and so I must be very careful. When Oz gives me a heart of course I needn't mind so much."

THE OUTLAWS OF SHERWOOD FOREST

FROM *THE ADVENTURES OF ROBIN HOOD*

ROGER LANCELYN GREEN

Early next morning Sir Guy of Gisborne set out for Arlingford Castle, his guide being the fat friar called Brother Michael who had so disgraced himself on the previous night by praising the outlawed Robin Hood.

The friar rode at his side singing lustily–in spite of the fact that as they left the Abbey, the Abbot had banished him in no uncertain terms: "You go out, false and traitorous man, as you came in many years ago: Plain Michael Tuck, no longer a Brother of this Order. If you show your face at my doors again, my doors will be shut in your face!"

"Why then!" cried the Friar gaily, "farewell to the Abbey of Fountains, and all hail to the jolly greenwood–and catch me again if you can!"

So he went on his way, singing:

For hark! hark! hark!
The dog doth bark,
That watches the wild deer's lair,
The hunter awakes at the peep of the dawn,

But the lair it is empty, the deer it is gone,
And the hunter knows not where!

As they came in sight of Arlingford Castle the Friar ceased from his singing, and turning to Sir Guy, remarked:

"You had best turn back, sir knight–or at the least lower that vizor of yours!"

"How?" exclaimed Guy of Gisborne. "Surely Lord Fitzwalter is not in league with Robin Hood?"

"Far from it!" laughed the fat Friar, "but Lady Marian Fitzwalter assuredly is. And Lady Marian is as apt with an arrow as most damsels are with a needle!"

They reached the castle in safety, however, and Lord Fitzwalter welcomed them loudly, showing great eagerness to be on the side in power:

"You have done me a wrong? How so? Would you have had me marry my daughter to an outlaw, a fly-by-night, a slayer of the King's deer–and of the Prince's followers? A man who flings away an earldom, broad lands and rich treasures to help a lot of miserable serfs and other riff-raff most justly persecuted by the laws of the land. No, sir, no: you have done me a service. A great service. I have finished with Fitzooth, or Robin Hood, or whatever that rascally beggar now calls himself. And so has my daughter."

"And yet she is half wedded to him by the dictates of the church," remarked the Friar, "and wholly his by the dictates of her heart."

"The marriage was not completed!" shouted Lord Fitzwalter. "Therefore I care nothing for it. As for love–it is your business, as her confessor, to show her that her love for this traitor is sinful and to be stamped out!"

"Marriages," quoth the Friar, "are made in Heaven. Love is God's work–and it is not for me to meddle with it."

"The ceremony was cut short–sure proof that Heaven laid no blessing on it!" roared Lord Fitzwalter. "Besides, I betrothed my daughter to the Earl of Huntingdon, not to the outlawed traitor Robin Hood."

"He may be pardoned," answered the Friar. "Coeur de Lion is a worthy king–and Fitzooth a worthy peer."

"There can be no pardon," said Sir Guy hastily. "He has killed the king's subjects and defied the king's sheriff."

Lord Fitzwalter was growing more and more red in the face with fury, but at this moment the Lady Marian came suddenly into the room, clad in Lincoln green, with a quiver of arrows at her side and a bow in her hand.

"How now?" roared her father. "Where are you off to now, wench?"

"To the greenwood," said Marian calmly.

"That you shall not!" bellowed Lord Fitzwalter.

"But I am going," said Marian.

"But I will have up the drawbridge."

"But I will swim the moat."

"But I will secure the gates."

"But I will leap from the battlement."

"But I will lock you in an upper chamber."

"But I will shred the tapestry and let myself down."

"But I will lock you in a turret where you shall only see light through a loophole."

"But I will find some way of escape. And, father, while I go freely, I shall return willingly. But once shut me up, and if I slip out then, I shall not return at all . . . Robin waits for me in the greenwood, and the knot half-tied yesterday can so easily be tied completely."

"Well spoken, lady," cried the Friar.

"Ill spoken, Friar!" thundered Lord Fitzwalter. "Get out of my castle this instant! You are in league with the traitor Robin Hood, I know it! If you come here again, I'll have you whipped, monk or no monk!"

"I go, I go!" said the Friar calmly. "I know of a hermitage by the riverside where I may well take up my abode–and levy toll on all those who would pass by: payment, of course, for my prayers! Abbey and castle have cast me out, but not so easily shall Friar Tuck be cast down!"

And away he strode, singing blithely:

For I must seek some hermit cell,
Where I alone my beads may tell,
And on the wight who that way fares
Levy a toll for my ghostly pray'rs!

"So much for an impudent friar!" puffed Lord Fitzwalter. "Now for a wayward girl!"

"A husband," said Sir Guy with meaning, "is the best curb for such as she."

"Aye, a husband–and of my choosing!" agreed Lord Fitzwalter. "No more earls of doubtful earldoms, but, shall we say, a knight with definite lands and treasures, and definitely in favor with Prince John! Such a man, in fact, as–well, no matter!'

Lord Fitzwalter looked Guy of Gisborne up and down with approval, but Marian broke out:

"No man of your choosing, father–unless he be my choice also. And my choice is and will ever be for brave Robin Hood!"

"I'll keep you in a dungeon and feed you on bread and water!" thundered Lord Fitzwalter.

"Robin will sack your castle to rescue me," said Marian gaily. Then suddenly serious, she exclaimed: "Father, you will let me go to the greenwood? You have my promise that I will return. And I promise also that Robin shall be nothing more to me than he is now, without your leave–or until King Richard return and give me to him in marriage with his own hand."

Then, blowing a kiss to her father, and paying no attention whatsoever to Guy of Gisborne, Marian tripped gaily from the room and away into Sherwood Forest.

"And now," said Lord Fitzwalter grimly, "it is for you to catch this outlaw and string him up to the highest gallows in Nottinghamshire. Until that is done, I fear there will be no use in your coming here to ask my daughter's hand in marriage."

Sir Guy rose and bowed to his host.

"My lord," he said, "I am already on my way to Locksley Hall. The Sheriff's men were to surround it last night, taking prisoner any who came in or out, and my followers do but await me at the Abbey. When I get there, it may well be to find Robin Hood already in their hands."

But Robert Fitzooth had not been so unaware of the dangers into which his double life as Robin Hood was leading him as the Sheriff and Prince John had supposed. When he escaped from the chapel after the interrupted wedding, Robin and some twenty men at arms rode off into Sherwood Forest and continued on their way to within a mile or so of Locksley Hall. Here Robin halted and turning, spoke to his followers:

"My friends, what I feared has befallen me. You all heard the mandate of outlawry read against me–and some of you may have incurred danger of the same by withstanding those men sent against me under Sir Guy of Gisborne. Well now, you may choose for yourselves: I set you all free from my service–but indeed as I am an outlaw, that sets you free whether I will or no. If you did not all know it already, you know now that I am that Robin Hood who, for several years now, has befriended all such as suffer under the cruelty and unjustness of lords, barons, bishops, abbots, and sheriffs. I have already a band of men sworn to follow me who await me in the greenwood: We are all comrades and brothers, though me they have chosen to be their leader and their king–not because I am by right an Earl, not merely because I have the gift of a steady hand and a clear eye and so can shoot an arrow further and straighter than most men, but because one must rule and I come of a race of rulers (though we are but slaves now to our Norman masters). I am no more Robert Fitzooth, Earl of Huntingdon, but the plain yeoman of Locksley whom men call Robin Hood: but my friends in Sherwood have chosen me king, and a king in Sherwood I shall be, my first care for my followers, but our first care for justice and mercy and the Love of God. And in this I hold that we commit no treason: When Richard comes home from the Crusade this reign of terror and of evil against which I fight will end. Cruel, lawless John will oppress us no longer, nor his friends and followers use us without right or justice, as slaves and not as free men.

"Choose now; will you follow me into Sherwood, all such of you as have neither wife nor child–or, as you blamelessly may, go back to serve the new master of Locksley? Only, for the love and service that was between us, I charge you to betray neither me nor any who were your companions and are now mine."

Then most of the men at arms cried aloud that they would follow Robin Hood through weal and woe, and all swore that they would die rather than betray him. Some then turned and with bent heads rode off towards Locksley–drawn thither by wife or child–and swore reluctantly to serve Sir Guy of Gisborne so long as he might be the master of Locksley.

"And now," said Robin to those who remained with him, "let us away to our new home in the forest and see how many of us there be who stand loyally together for God, for His anointed servant Richard, King by right divine, and for justice and the righting of wrongs."

Deep in the heart of Sherwood Forest, as the sun was setting behind them, Robin and his men came to a great glade where stood the greatest of all the forest oaks upon a stretch of open greensward with steep banks fencing it on either hand in which were caves both deep and dry. At either end of the shallow valley, and beyond the banks on each side, the forest hedged them in with its mighty trees, with oak and ash, with beech and elm and chestnut, and also with thick clumps of impassable thorns, with desolate marshes where an unwary step might catch a man or a horse and drag him down into the dark quagmire, and with brambles rising like high dykes and knolls through which even a man in armor could scarcely force his way.

For the last mile Robin led by narrow, winding paths, pointing out to his companions the secret, hidden signs by which they could find their way.

Once in the glade, Robin took the horn from his belt and blew on it a blast which echoed away and away into the distance. Already men dressed smartly in doublet and hose of Lincoln green, in hoods of green or russet and in knee-boots of soft brown leather, had come out from the caves to greet them.

At a few brief words, they set about lighting two great fires near the oak tree in the glade, and roasting great joints of venison before them. They also brought coarse loaves of brown bread, and rolled out two barrels of ale, setting up rough trestle tables with logs in lieu of stools.

As the darkness grew, men kept appearing silently in the glade and taking their place by the fires or at the tables until a company of fifty or sixty was gathered together.

Then Robin Hood rose up and addressed them. He began by telling them, as he had told the men at arms, of his banishment, and reminding them that they were outlaws, but not robbers.

"We must take the King's deer," he ended, "since we must eat to live. But when the King returns I myself will beg pardon at his feet for this trespass. And now you shall all swear the oath which I swear with you, and all seeking to join us must swear also. We declare war upon all of those thieves, robbers, extortioners, and men of evil whom we find among the nobles, the clergy, and burgesses of town–in particular those who follow or accompany Prince John; false abbots, monks, bishops, and archbishops, whom we will beat and bind like sheaves of corn so that they may yield the golden grain of their robberies–the Abbots of St. Mary's, Doncaster, and Fountains shall we seek for in particular; and I think we shall keep within our oath if we make it our especial care to harry and persecute the false Sheriff of Nottingham who so wickedly abuses his power to please and satisfy his master Prince John.

"Now, my friends, we do not take from these and their kind to enrich ourselves. We take for the general good, and it shall be as much our duty to seek out the poor, the needy, the widow, the orphan and all those who have suffered or are suffering wrong, and minister to their wants in so far as we can.

"We shall swear, moreover, to harm no woman, be she Norman or Saxon, high or low, but to assist any who crave our aid or need our protection, dealing with them with all honesty and purity, seeing in every woman the likeness of Our Lady the Holy Mary, Mother of Christ."

Then, in that wild and lonely glade, while the owls screamed over the dark forest, and an occasional wolf howled in the distance, they all knelt down together and swore their oath–a pledge as high and sacred, though they were but outlaws and escaped felons, as that sworn by the noblest knight who, in the days when the Saxons themselves were the conquerors and oppressors, had sat at King Arthur's Table.

THE HARE AND THE TORTOISE

AESOP

The hare was once boasting of his speed before the other animals. "I have never yet been beaten," said he, "when I put forth my full speed. I challenge anyone here to race with me."

The Tortoise said quietly, "I accept your challenge."

"That is a good joke," said the Hare; "I could dance round you all the way."

"Save your boasting till you've won," answered the Tortoise. "Shall we race?"

So a course was fixed and a start was made. The Hare darted almost out of sight at once, but soon stopped and, to show his contempt for the Tortoise, lay down to have a nap. The Tortoise plodded on and plodded on, and when the Hare awoke from his nap, he saw the Tortoise just near the finish line and could not run up in time to save the race. Then said the Tortoise:

"Plodding wins the race."

The Miser and His Gold

Aesop

Once upon a time there was a Miser who hid his gold at the foot of a tree in his garden; but every week he would go and dig it up and gloat over his riches.

A robber, who had noticed this, went and dug up the gold and ran off with it. When the Miser next came to gloat over his treasure, he found nothing but the empty hole. He pulled his hair, and raised such an outcry that all the neighbors gathered around him, and he told them how he used to come and visit his gold.

"Did you ever take any of it out?" asked one of them.

"No," said he, "I only came to look at it."

"Then come again and look at the hole," said a neighbor; "it will do you just as much good."

"Wealth unused might as well not exist."

PUZZLES AND PUNS

How did the kids get wet on their way to school?

They were in a carpool.

Where does a frog get his eyes checked?

At the hop-tometrist!

A man started to town with a fox, a goose, and a sack of corn. He came to a stream that he had to cross in a tiny boat. He could only take one across at a time. He could not leave the fox alone with the goose or the goose alone with the corn. How did he get them all safely over the stream?

He took the goose over first and came back.
Then he took the fox across and brought the goose back.
Next he took the corn over. He came back alone and took the goose.

How do you spell Mississippi?

The River or the State?

Can you name the capital of every state
in America in less than 30 seconds?

Washington, D.C.

What animal walks on 4 feet in the
morning, 2 at noon, and 3 in the evening?

*Man. He crawls on all fours as a baby, walks on two feet
when he is grown, and uses a cane in his old age.*

Where do elderly eggs live?

In an old yolks home.

English Teacher: Today we will be discussing
The Hunchback of Notre Dame. Who can tell us
something about Quasimodo? Peter, can you?

Peter: No, but the name does ring a bell.

What holds water even though it is full of holes?

A sponge.

Which month has 28 days?

They all do!

Scrooge was sitting in his office in the week before Christmas. He was counting his money, making sure he had made enough profit for the year. Suddenly, he became aware of a noise. It was one of those irritating humming noises that once you've noticed it, you can't concentrate on anything else, so after some time trying to ignore it, he decided to investigate. He looked all around, and finally managed to pinpoint the sound coming from under his desk. Bending down to look under the desk, he was surprised to see Jiminy Cricket, playing a tune.

He crouched down, and said "Jiminy!" (for they already knew each other), "what are you doing?"

"I'm singing you a Christmas carol," Jiminy replied, "but I've forgotten the words, so I'm just humming it instead."

"That's not all," says Scrooge, "You're only playing the first bar, over and over again."

"Well," says Jiminy, "I guess that makes me a *bar hum bug.*"

What happens when a bird flies into something?

A wing ding.

Why did the zoo fire the owl?

He didn't give a hoot.

What is the difference between a dog and a gossip?

One has a wagging tail, the other a wagging tongue.

Why do you always find something in the last place you look?

Because when you find it, you stop looking.

What do you get when you cross a parrot and a centipede?

A walkie talkie!

Who gave the Liberty Bell to Philadelphia?
Must have been a family of ducks.
A family of ducks?
Yes. Didn't you say there was a *quack* in it?

Why did the jogger go to see the doctor?

He was feeling run down.

If I Were King

A.A. Milne

I often wish I were a King,
And then I could do anything.

If only I were King of Spain,
I'd take my hat off in the rain.

If only I were King of France,
I wouldn't brush my hair for aunts.

I think, if I were King of Greece,
I'd push things off the mantelpiece.

If I were King of Norroway,
I'd ask an elephant to stay.

If I were King of Babylon,
I'd leave my button gloves undone.

If I were King of Timbuctoo,
I'd think of lovely things to do.

If I were King of anything,
I'd tell the soldiers, "I'm the King!"

The Woman with the Golden Arm

Retold by Mark Twain

Once upon a time, long ago, there was a man and his wife that lived all alone in a house out in the middle of a big lonesome prairie. There wasn't anybody or any house or any trees for miles and miles and miles around. The woman had an arm that was gold–just pure solid gold from the shoulder all the way down.

Well, by and by, one night, she died. It was in the middle of the winter, and the wind was a-blowing, and the snow was a-drifting, and the sleet was a-driving, and it was awful dark; but the man had to bury her; so he took her, and took a lantern, and went away off across the prairie and dug a grave; but just when he was going to put her in, he thought he would steal her golden arm, for he judged it couldn't ever be found out, and he was a powerful mean man.

So then he cut it off, and buried her, and started back home. And he stumbled along, and plowed along, and the snow and the sleet swashed in his face so he had to turn his head to one side, and could hardly get along at all; and the wind it kept a-crying, and a-wailing, and a-mourning, way off across the prairie, back there where the grave was, just so: *B-z-z-z-z-z-z.* It seemed to him like it was a ghost crying and worrying about some trouble or another, and it made his hair stand up, and he was all trembling and shivering. The wind kept on going *B-z-z-z-z-z-z,* and all of a sudden he caught his breath and stood still, and leaned his ear to listen.

B-z-z-z-z-z-z goes the wind, but right along in the midst of that sound he hears some words, so faint and so far away off he can hardly make them out. *"W-h-e-r-e-'s m-y g-o-l-d-e-n a-a-a-arm? W-h-o's g-o-t m-y g-o-l-d-e-n a-a-a-arm?"*

Down drops the lantern; and out it goes, and there he is, in that wide lonesome prairie, in the pitch-dark and the storm. He started along again, but he could hardly pull one foot after the other; and all the way the wind was a-crying, and the snow a-blowing, and the voice was a-wailing, *"W-h-e-r-e's m-y g-o-l-d-e-n a-a-a-arm? W-h-o's g-o-t m-y g-o-l-d-e-n a-a-a-arm?"*

At last he got home; and he locked the door, and bolted it, and chained it with a big log chain and put the chairs and things against it; and then he crept upstairs, and got into bed, and covered up his head and ears, and lay there a-shivering and a-listening.

The wind it kept a-going *B-z-z-z-z,* and there was that voice again–away, *ever* so far away, out in the prairie. But it was a-coming–it was a-coming. Every time it said the words it was closer than it was before. By and by it was as close as the pasture; next it was as close as the branch; next it was this side of the branch and right by the corncrib; next it was to the smokehouse; then it was right at the stile; then right in the yard; then it passed the ash hopper and was right at the door–right at the very door!

"W-h-e-r-e's m-y g-o-l-d-e-n a-a-a-arm?" The man shook, and shook, and shivered. He don't hear the chain rattle, he don't hear the bolt break, he

don't hear the door move–still next minute he hears something coming *p-a-t, p-a-t, p-a-t,* just as slow, and just as soft, up the stairs. It's right at the door, now: *"W-h-e-r-e's m-y g-o-l-d-e-n a-a-a-arm?"*

Next it's right in the room: *"W-h-o's g-o-t m-y g-o-l-d-e-n a-a-a-arm?"*

Then it's right up against the bed–then it's a-leaning down over the bed–then it's down right against his ear and a-whispering so soft and dreadful: *"W-h-e-r-e's m-y g-o-l-d-e-n a-a-a-arm? W-h-o's g-o-t m-y g-o-l-d-e-n a-a-a-arm?"*

"YOU GOT IT!"

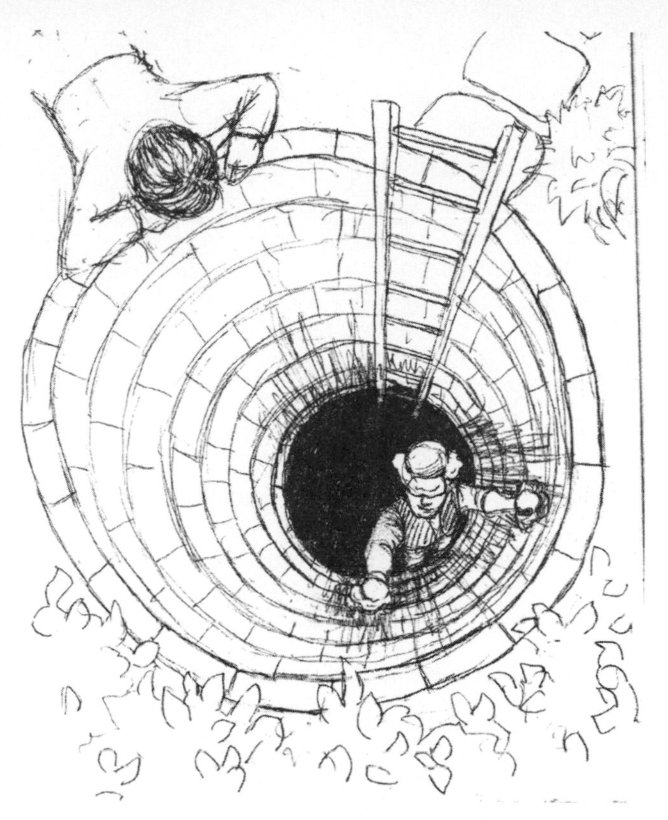

The Story of Jason Squiff and Why He Had a Popcorn Hat, Popcorn Mittens, and Popcorn Shoes

Carl Sandburg

Jason Squiff was a cistern cleaner. He had greenish yellowish hair. If you looked down into a cistern when he was lifting buckets of slush and mud you could tell where he was, you could pick him out down in the dark cistern, by the lights of his greenish yellowish hair.

Sometimes the buckets of slush and mud tipped over and ran down on the top of his head. This covered his greenish yellowish hair. And then it was hard to tell where he was and it was not easy to pick him out down in the dark where he was cleaning the cistern.

One day Jason Squiff came to the Bimber house and knocked on the door.

"Did I understand," he said, speaking to Mrs. Bimber, Blixie Bimber's mother, "do I understand you sent for me to clean the cistern in your backyard?"

"You understand exactly such," said Mrs. Bimber, "and you are welcome as the flowers that bloom in the spring, tra-la-la."

"Then I will go to work and clean the cistern, tra-la-la," he answered, speaking to Mrs. Bimber. "I'm the guy, tra-la-la," he said further, running his excellent fingers through his greenish yellowish hair, which was shining brightly.

He began cleaning the cistern. Blixie Bimber came out in the backyard. She looked down in the cistern. It was all dark. It looked like nothing but all dark down there. By and by she saw something greenish yellowish. She watched it. Soon she saw it was Jason Squiff's head and hair. And then she knew the cistern was being cleaned and Jason Squiff was on the job. So she sang tra-la-la and went back into the house and told her mother Jason Squiff was on the job.

The last bucketful of slush and mud came at last for Jason Squiff. He squinted at the bottom. Something was shining. He reached his fingers down through the slush and mud and took out what was shining.

It was the gold buckskin whincher Blixie Bimber lost from the gold chain around her neck the week before when she was looking down into the cistern to see what she could see. It was exactly the same gold buckskin whincher shining and glittering like a sign of happiness.

"It's luck," said Jason Squiff, wiping his fingers on his greenish yellowish hair. Then he put the gold buckskin whincher in his vest pocket and spoke to himself again, "It's luck."

A little after six o'clock that night Jason Squiff stepped into his house and home and said hello to his wife and daughters. They all began to laugh. Their laughter was a ticklish laughter.

"Something funny is happening," he said.

"And you are it," they all laughed at him again with ticklish laughter.

Then they showed him. His hat was popcorn, his mittens popcorn, and his shoes popcorn. He didn't know the gold buckskin whincher had a power and was working all the time. He didn't know the whincher in his vest pocket was saying, "You have a letter Q in your name and because you have the pleasure and happiness of having a Q in your name you must have a popcorn hat, popcorn mittens and popcorn shoes."

The next morning he put on another hat, another pair of mittens and another pair of shoes. And the minute he put them on they changed to popcorn.

So he tried on all his hats, mittens and shoes. Always they changed to popcorn the minute he had them on.

He went downtown to the stores. He bought a new hat, mittens and shoes. And the minute he had them on they changed to popcorn.

So he decided he would go to work and clean cisterns with his popcorn hat, popcorn mittens and popcorn shoes on.

The people of the Village of Cream Puffs enjoyed watching him walk up the street, going to clean cisterns. People five and six blocks away could see him coming and going with his popcorn hat, popcorn mittens, and popcorn shoes.

When he was down in a cistern the children enjoyed looking down into the cistern to see him work. When none of the slush and mud fell on his hat and mittens he was easy to find. The light of the shining popcorn lit up the whole inside of the cistern.

Sometimes, of course, the white popcorn got full of black slush and black mud. And then when Jason Squiff came up and walked home he was not quite so dazzling to look at.

It was a funny winter for Jason Squiff.

"It's a crime, a dirty crime," he said to himself. "Now I can never be alone with my thoughts. Everybody looks at me when I go up the street. If I meet a funeral even the pall bearers begin to laugh at my popcorn hat. If I meet people going to a wedding they throw all the rice at me as if I am a bride and a groom all together. The horses try to eat my hat wherever I go. Three hats I have fed to horses this winter. And if I accidentally drop one of my mittens the chickens eat it."

Then Jason Squiff began to change. He became proud.

"I always wanted a beautiful hat like this white popcorn hat," he said to himself. "And I always wanted white beautiful mittens and white beautiful shoes like these white popcorn mittens and shoes."

When the boys yelled, "Snow man! Yah-de-dah-de-dah, Snow man!" he just waved his hand to them with an upward gesture of his arm to show he was proud of how he looked.

"They all watch for me," he said to himself, "I am distinguished–am I not?" he asked himself.

And he put his right hand into his left hand and shook hands with himself and said, "You certainly look fixed up."

One day he decided to throw away his vest. In the vest pocket was the gold buckskin whincher, with the power working, the power saying, "You have a letter Q in your name and because you have the pleasure and happiness of having a Q in your name you must have a popcorn hat, popcorn mittens, and popcorn shoes."

Yes, he threw away the vest. He forgot all about the gold buckskin whincher being in the vest.

He just handed the vest to a rag man. And the rag man put the vest with the gold buckskin whincher in a bag on his back and walked away.

After that Jason Squiff was like other people. His hats would never change to popcorn nor his mittens to popcorn nor his shoes to popcorn.

And when anybody looked at him down in a cistern cleaning the cistern or when anybody saw him walking along the street they knew him by his greenish yellowish hair which was always full of bright lights.

And so–if you have a Q in your name, be careful if you ever come across a gold buckskin whincher. Remember different whinchers have different powers.

The Inventing Room—Everlasting Gobstoppers and Hair Toffee

From *Charlie and the Chocolate Factory*

Roald Dahl

When Mr. Wonka shouted "Stop the boat!" the Oompa-Loompas jammed their oars into the river and backed water furiously. The boat stopped.

The Oompa-Loompas guided the boat alongside the red door. On the door it said, INVENTING ROOM–PRIVATE–KEEP OUT. Mr. Wonka took a key from his pocket, leaned over the side of the boat, and put the key in the keyhole.

"*This* is the most important room in the entire factory!" he said. "All my most secret new inventions are cooking and simmering in here! Old Fickelgruber would give his front teeth to be allowed inside just for three minutes! So would Prodnose and Slugworth and all the other rotten chocolate makers! But now, listen to me! I want no messing about when you go in! No touching, no meddling, and no tasting! Is that agreed?"

"Yes, yes!" the children cried. "We won't touch a thing!"

"Up to now," Mr. Wonka said, "nobody else, not even an Oompa-Loompa, has ever been allowed in here!" He opened the door and stepped out of the boat into the room. The four children and their parents all scrambled after him.

"Don't touch!" shouted Mr. Wonka. "And don't knock anything over!"

Charlie Bucket stared around the gigantic room in which he now found himself. The place was like a witch's kitchen! All about him black metal pots were boiling and bubbling on huge stoves, and kettles were hissing and pans were sizzling, and strange iron machines were clanking and spluttering, and there were pipes running all over the ceiling and walls, and the whole place was filled with smoke and steam and delicious rich smells.

Mr. Wonka himself had suddenly become even more excited than usual, and anyone could see that this was the room he loved best of all. He was hopping about among the saucepans and the machines like a child among his Christmas presents, not knowing which thing to look at first. He lifted the lid from a huge pot and took a sniff; then he rushed over and dipped a finger into a barrel of sticky yellow stuff and had a taste; then he skipped across to one of the machines and turned half a dozen knobs this way and that; then he peered anxiously through the glass door of a gigantic oven, rubbing his hands and cackling with delight at what he saw inside. Then he ran over to another machine, a small shiny affair that kept going *phut-phut-phut-phut-phut,* and every time it went *phut,* a large green marble dropped out of it into a basket on the floor. At least it looked like a marble.

"Everlasting Gobstoppers!" cried Mr. Wonka proudly. "They're completely new! I am inventing them for children who are given very little pocket money. You can put an Everlasting Gobstopper in your mouth and you can suck it and suck it and suck it and it will *never* get any smaller!"

"It's like gum!" cried Violet Beauregarde.

"It is *not* like gum," Mr. Wonka said. "Gum is for chewing, and if you tried chewing one of these Gobstoppers here you'd break your teeth off. But they taste terrific! And they change color once a week! And they *never* get any smaller! They *never* disappear! *NEVER!* At least I don't think they do. There's one of them being tested this very moment in the Testing Room next door. An Oompa-Loompa is sucking it. He's been sucking it for very nearly a year now without stopping, and it's still just as good as ever!

"Now, over here," Mr. Wonka went on, skipping excitedly across the room to the opposite wall, "over here I am inventing a completely new line in toffees!" He stopped beside a large saucepan. The saucepan was full of a thick gooey purplish treacle, boiling and bubbling. By standing on his toes, little Charlie could just see inside it.

"That's Hair Toffee!" cried Mr. Wonka. "You eat just one tiny bit of that, and in exactly half an hour a brand-new luscious thick silky beautiful crop of hair will start growing out all over the top of your head! And a moustache! And a beard!"

"A beard!" cried Veruca Salt. "Who wants a beard, for heaven's sake?"

"It would suit you very well," said Mr. Wonka, "but unfortunately the mixture is not quite right yet. I've got it too strong. It works too well. I tried it on an Oompa-Loompa yesterday in the Testing Room and immediately a huge beard started shooting out of his chin, and the beard grew so fast that soon it was trailing all over the floor in a thick hairy carpet. It was growing faster than we could cut it! In the end we had to use a lawn mower to keep it in check! But I'll get the mixture right soon! And when I do, then there'll be no excuse any more for little boys and girls going about with bald heads!"

"But Mr. Wonka," said Mike Teavee, "little boys and girls never *do* go about with. . . ."

"Don't argue, my dear child, *please* don't argue!" cried Mr. Wonka. "It's such a waste of precious time!"

Daniel Boone

Arthur Guiterman

Daniel Boone at twenty-one
Came with his tomahawk, knife, and gun
Home from the French and Indian War
To North Carolina and the Yadkin shore.
He married his maid with a golden band,
Builded his house and cleared his land;
But the deep woods claimed their son again
And he turned his face from the homes of men.
Over the Blue Ridge, dark and lone,
The Mountains of Iron, the Hills of Stone,
Braving the Shawnee's jealous wrath,

He made his way on the Warrior's Path.
Alone he trod the shadowed trails;
But he was lord of a thousand vales
As he roved Kentucky, far and near,
Hunting the buffalo, elk and deer.
What joy to see, what joy to win
So fair a land for his kith and kin,
Of streams unstained and woods unhewn!
"Elbow room!" laughed Daniel Boone.

On the Wilderness Road that his axmen made
The settlers flocked to the first stockade;
The deerskin shirts and the coonskin caps
Filed through the glens and the mountain gaps;
And hearts were high in the fateful spring
When the land said "Nay!" to the stubborn king.
While the men of the East of farm and town
Strove with the troops of the British Crown,
Daniel Boone from a surge of hate
Guarded a nation's westward gate.
Down in the fort in a wave of flame
The Shawnee horde and the Mingo came,
And the stout logs shook in a storm of lead;
But Boone stood firm and the savage fled.

Peace! And the settlers flocked anew,
The farm lands spread, and the town lands grew;
But Daniel Boone was ill at ease
When he saw the smoke in his forest trees.
"There'll be no game in the country soon.
Elbow room!" cried Daniel Boone.

Straight as a pine at sixty-five–
Time enough for a man to thrive–
He launched his bateau on Ohio's breast
And his heart was glad as he oared it west;
There was kindly folk and his own true blood
Where the great Missouri rolls his flood;
New woods, new streams, and room to spare,
And Daniel Boone found comfort there.
Yet far he ranged toward the sunset still,
Where the Kansas runs and the Smoky Hill,
And the prairies toss, by the south wind blown;
And he killed his bear on the Yellowstone.
But ever he dreamed of new domains
With vaster woods and wider plains;
Ever he dreamed of a world-to-be
Where there are no bounds and the soul is free.
At fourscore-five, still stout and hale,

He heard a call to a farther trail;
So he turned his face where the stars are strewn;
"Elbow room!" sighed Daniel Boone.

Down the Milky Way in its banks of blue
Far he has paddled his white canoe
To the splendid quest of the tameless soul–
He has reached the goal where there is no goal.
Now he rides and rides an endless trail
On the hippogriff of the flaming tail
Or the horse of the stars with the golden mane
As he rode the first of the blue-grass strain.
The joy that lies in the search he seeks
On breathless hills with crystal peaks;
He makes his camp on heights untrod,
The steps of the shrine, alone with God.
Through the woods of the vast, on the plains of space
He hunts the pride of the mammoth race
And the dinosaur of the triple horn,
The manticore and the unicorn,
As once by the broad Missouri's flow
He followed the elk and the buffalo.
East of the sun and west of the moon,
"Elbow room!" laughs Daniel Boone.

In the Dark

A.A. Milne

I've had my supper,
    And *had* my supper,
        And HAD my supper and all;
I've heard the story
    Of Cinderella,
        And how she went to the ball;
I've cleaned my teeth,
    And I've said my prayers,
        And I've cleaned and said them right;
And they've all of them been
    And kissed me lots,
        They've all of them said "Good-night."
So–here I am in the dark alone,
    There's nobody here to see;
        I think to myself,
        I play to myself,
    And nobody knows what I say to myself;
Here I am in the dark alone,
    What is it going to be?

I can think whatever I like to think,
I can play whatever I like to play,
I can laugh whatever I like to laugh,
There's nobody here but me.

I'm talking to a rabbit . . .
I'm talking to the sun . . .
I think I am a hundred–
I'm one.
I'm lying in a forest . . .
I'm lying in a cave . . .
I'm talking to a Dragon . . .
I'm BRAVE.
I'm lying on my left side . . .
I'm lying on my right . . .
I'll play a lot tomorrow . . .
. . . .
I'll think a lot tomorrow . . .
. . . .
I'll laugh . . .
a lot . . .
tomorrow . . .
(Heigh-ho!)
Good night.

Author Index